Cristina shifted. "No."

Her hesitation gave him a different answer, but Gabriel wouldn't call her on it. Not yet. "All right."

He found it endearing, the way surprise and disappointment washed across her face before she stepped back. What an innocent she was. If her father played his cards right—the emotional ones— she'd marry the man he'd chosen for her. For her father's sake, of course, not hers. She believed in love—or the fantasy of love. But she also believed in family.

He, on the other hand, had never allowed family to dictate his life, except once. He had promised his mother he wouldn't exact revenge against his father, even though the opportunity and means had been within Gabe's reach many times. What was the purpose of having money and the power that came with it if he couldn't use it as he wished?

Wasn't that the reason he was seducing Cristina? He couldn't allow himself to think of any other.

Dear Reader,

August predictably brings long steamy days…and hot sensuous nights. And this month Silhouette Desire spotlights the kind of pure passion that can erupt only in that sizzling summer climate.

Get ready to fall head over heels for August's MAN OF THE MONTH, a sexy rancher who opens his home (and his heart?) to a lost beauty desperately hoping to recover her memory in *A Montana Man* by Jackie Merritt. Bestselling author Cait London continues her hugely popular miniseries THE TALLCHIEFS with *Rafe Palladin: Man of Secrets*. Rafe is an irresistible takeover tycoon with a plan to *acquire* a Tallchief lady. Barbara McMahon brings readers the second story in her IDENTICAL TWINS! duo—in *The Older Man* an exuberant young woman is swept up by her love and desire for a tremendously gorgeous, *much* older man.

Plus, talented Susan Crosby unfolds a story of seduction, revenge and scandal in the continuation of THE LONE WOLVES with *His Seductive Revenge*. And TEXAS BRIDES are back with *The Restless Virgin* by Peggy Moreland, the story of an innocent Western lady tired of waiting around for marriage—so she lassos herself one unsuspecting cowboy! And you've never seen a hero like *The Consummate Cowboy,* by Sara Orwig. He's all man, all-around ornery and all-out tempted…by his ex-wife's sister!

I know you'll enjoy reading all six of this sultry month's brand-new Silhouette Desire novels by some of the most beloved and sexy authors of romance.

Regards,

Melissa Senate

Melissa Senate
Senior Editor
Silhouette Books

Please address questions and book requests to:
Silhouette Reader Service
U.S.: 3010 Walden Ave., P.O. Box 1325, Buffalo, NY 14269
Canadian: P.O. Box 609, Fort Erie, Ont. L2A 5X3

SUSAN CROSBY
HIS SEDUCTIVE REVENGE

SILHOUETTE *Desire*®

Published by Silhouette Books

America's Publisher of Contemporary Romance

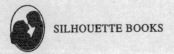

SILHOUETTE BOOKS

ISBN 0-373-76162-7

HIS SEDUCTIVE REVENGE

Copyright © 1998 by Susan Bova Crosby

This edition published by arrangement with Harlequin Books S.A.

Printed in U.S.A.

Books by Susan Crosby

Silhouette Desire

The Mating Game #888
Almost a Honeymoon #952
Baby Fever #1018
Wedding Fever #1061
Marriage on His Mind #1108
Bride Candidate #9 #1131
*His Most Scandalous Secret #1158
*His Seductive Revenge #1162

*The Lone Wolves

SUSAN CROSBY

is fascinated by the special and complex communication of courtship, and so she burrows into her office to dream up warm, strong heroes and good-hearted, self-reliant heroines to satisfy her own love of happy endings.

She and her husband have two grown sons and live in the Central Valley of California. She spent a mere seven and a half years getting through college and finally earned a B.A. in English a few years ago. She has worked as a synchronized swimming instructor, a personnel interviewer at a toy factory, and a trucking company manager. Involved for many years behind the scenes in a local community theater, she has made only one stage appearance—as the rear end of a camel! Variety, she says, makes for more interesting novels.

Readers are welcome to write to her at P.O. Box 1836, Lodi, CA 95241.

For Elizabeth Bova, my guiding light.
Thanks for showing me the way.
I miss you, Mom.

Prologue

"**H**e's selling his daughter?" Gabriel Marquez leaned forward. His gaze drilled the man seated across his mahogany desk. "Cristina Chandler's father made a deal to exchange her hand in marriage for *cash?*"

"Enough cash to keep him out of bankruptcy court, and then some," the man called Doc replied. "And to avoid public humiliation, of course. A Chandler without money? It would be too embarrassing."

"The Chandlers have lived on reputation, not real money, for a long time. Is she aware she's being bartered?"

"I doubt it. She just moved out of the family mansion and into her own apartment." Doc tossed a stack of papers on the desk. "Plus, the prenuptial agreement has been drawn up but not signed, as you can see. That second set of documents is a separate contract between the men, spelling out their own deal. It's obvious they're scrambling. Everything's falling apart. They can't prove what caused the accident, so all they can do at this point is damage control. You know the drill—act as if nothing's wrong and people believe it. The longer your friend

Sebastian is out of the picture, the more he seems responsible, not them.''

Gabe dragged the documents closer. He knew exactly where the responsibility—and the blame—fell. ''Grimes's son must be in on the deal. He'll have to propose to the woman.''

''Who knows how much he's been told? He's not involved in the daily operations of the business, but he and Ms. Chandler have been seen together a lot lately. They've also known each other since childhood. Unfortunately, we may not know if the plan's a success until an engagement announcement hits the newspapers.''

''Which I must prevent.'' Gabe was buying time. Time for Sebastian to prove his innocence and reclaim his honor, as he'd demanded. Physically he couldn't defend himself yet.

Gabe thumbed through the papers. The prenup seemed basic for anyone protecting millions, the deal between the fathers brutally specific. But former Senator Chandler was accustomed to using power, and Richard Grimes to abusing it. ''How did you get these?''

''You don't want to know.''

''No one can trace you to me?''

''Has anyone before?''

Gabe studied the man who moved in and out of the city shadows with quiet efficiency, a specialist at what he did, hence the nickname Doc. Little shocked Gabe anymore, but a man selling his own daughter— He shut down the thought.

He thanked Doc, dismissing him, then he linked his fingers behind his head, leaned back and closed his eyes, savoring the anticipation that coursed through him. Sebastian would have his day—and the guilt that walked, talked and slept with Gabe in ever-deepening darkness since the accident would fade. He had involved Sebastian in his need for revenge, a need handcuffed by a promise. Taking down Richard Grimes and Arthur Chandler would help to ease the guilt. It would definitely help. Sebastian would pound the final nails in their coffins, but Gabe would dig the graves.

Unable to sit still, he picked up a photograph that Doc had brought, then walked the generous confines of the office that took up half the second story of his home. Dispassionately he studied the black-and-white photo of the woman about to be sold into marriage. Cristina Chandler. Her hair was a medium tone, and long enough to be banded in a ponytail while she played tennis at the country club. Her eyes were light—blue, probably. Her body was…unremarkable. The typical well-toned, angular body of a well-bred debutante—former debutante. She was twenty-seven years old, according to the fact sheet stapled to the photo. Graduated with respectable grades from a local state college, majored in computer graphics. Mother died two years ago. No siblings. No job. Recently leased an apartment in the city.

Just another woman of privilege, as cool as she was sleek. He knew her type, had avoided her type all his life.

He stopped pacing in front of the large De La Hoya portrait of his mother. He'd regretted the promise he'd made to her seventeen years ago, regretted it so much he hadn't made a promise to anyone except Sebastian since then. Circumstances change with time. At fifteen, he hadn't known that yet. Now, at thirty-two, he knew better. And he knew he had to break that early promise.

The time had come. As if preordained, everything was falling into place. Nothing could stop what would happen now. Preventing this merger that the families were calling a marriage was the first step.

Gabe moved to look out a window. The city skyline was shrouded with morning fog, the kind that would burn off soon, revealing a crisp San Francisco autumn day. It suited his mood, for a fog was surely lifting from his own life. Richard Grimes and Arthur Chandler would pay for what they'd done.

The sins of the fathers are to be laid upon the children.

The quotation rang in Gabe's head. A price would be exacted between the generations, a price long overdue, in Gabe's book. Yet there would be other costs. His mother may never forgive him, even though he also sought justice for her. And Miss Cristina Chandler may find herself an inadvertent victim of convenience—Gabe's, and the other men's. But the world needed to hear the truth, and perhaps the cool, sophisticated woman was due to have her eyes opened, as well. Perhaps he was even saving her from a worse fate.

He could not fail. He'd waited a long time for this moment, and indeed, there would be a price to pay. But reward justified risk. That was his motto.

One

"There's something wonderfully visceral about his work, don't you think?" Cristina Chandler pressed her wineglass to her lips as she tried to understand her intense reaction to the painting in front of her. The Galeria Secreto teemed with people, but the voices were hushed and the laughter low, almost seductive, as if the tone had been established by the display they were all there to see—the newest De La Hoya creations.

What incredible work it was. Big canvas, broad strokes, bold colors, seething with passion. She couldn't recall ever viewing a nude painted with such fire, such blatant sexuality, and yet it was tasteful enough to hang in a living room, although it certainly belonged in the privacy of someone's bedroom.

"Makes you wonder if the artist fooled around with her," Jen Wilding said under her breath. "I mean, look at her face. If that isn't a well-satisfied woman, I don't know what is."

Cristina slid her glass across her lips again. "I don't know that she's satisfied. Not yet. I think she's been thoroughly aroused, and satisfaction is just moments away."

"And your father has commissioned your portrait from this De La Hoya person? Has he ever seen this guy's work? Does he know you'd have to spend time alone with him?"

A picture started to form in Cristina's mind as she imagined what Alejandro De La Hoya looked like. Dark, undoubtedly. Latin. With intense eyes that looked deep inside a person and drew out their fantasies. A man who would see through lies and insecurities to what was real. A man for whom a woman would gladly strip herself bare and not feel the least bit shy. Or hesitant. Or humiliated.

Jen whimpered. Cristina smiled at her friend.

"God, Cris, I'm getting hot just thinking about taking that woman's place." Jen drained her wineglass and set it on the tray of a passing waiter, grabbing a full one with the other hand in a practiced move. "It's been weeks since I tangled under the sheets with anyone."

Weeks? Cristina thought as they moved on. *I should be so lucky.* "What if De La Hoya is eighty years old and has a wart on his nose?"

"I'd shut my eyes. Any man who could make me feel like that woman obviously does— But if he looked like *that* I'd be ecstatic," Jen said as she stopped at the next painting.

Cristina glanced at the program in her hand, looking for the title of the portrait Jen was panting over. *Sebastian.* The name teased her memory, the reason just beyond her grasp, but perhaps only because it was an old-fashioned name for such a modern man. And yet it suited him. His long, black hair framed a solid face with fine, dark eyes and a hard mouth, the image of a lord from another land, another century—who wore jeans, a lumberjack shirt and boots. Definitely twentieth century stuff.

Jen sighed. "I'll bet he'd have *me* shouting timber more than once a night."

Cristina laughed. She was glad she'd come, after all. She'd almost ignored the out-of-the-blue, engraved invitation, probably would have, except that Jen refused to let her. Too many strange things had happened lately, and she needed an evening of pure fun.

"So, what's the deal with this portrait your dad is arranging?" Jen asked. "I know that De La Hoya is all the rage, but isn't he, like, superexpensive?"

"Not only expensive, but incredibly mysterious. No one ever sees him."

"How is that possible?"

"The rumor is that he works behind some sort of curtain or two-way mirror. I don't know the specifics. Anyway, it doesn't matter. Even if De La Hoya agrees, I'm not going to allow it. I don't think Father can afford to spend that kind of money, even if it does complete the family gallery. Besides which, it just seems so pretentious."

"That is often the point, I believe," said a man from behind them, his voice as hushed and seductive as the environment demanded.

Cristina and Jen turned. He'd obviously been eavesdropping on their conversation.

"Pretension is the point?" Cristina asked. His eyes mesmerized her, their dark, glittering depths pulling her in, stopping her breath. *Not quite civilized.* The thought flashed in her mind, fizzled, then flared again even brighter when he moved a little closer. She watched his mouth as he spoke.

"Don't you believe we buy art not only for how it makes us feel, but for how our friends will react?" he asked.

"No." His lips looked soft and firm. She almost touched them. "Art is very personal to me," she added.

He made the slightest shift in his stance, as if a soldier at attention had been ordered at ease. "Gabriel Marquez," he said, extending his hand.

"Cristina Chandler."

"And I'm Jen, the ignored one. I'm here, too. Although you two sure couldn't tell it the last couple of minutes," she grumbled. "I'm going to feed my noisy and empty stomach, Cris. Do you want anything?"

Cristina shook her head, taking an unobtrusive step back at the same time. He was crowding her space, and she needed breathing room. "I'm to assume that you have a collection of art you've bought merely to shock or pacify your fri she asked, then sipped her wine, giving herself a moment to admire him, from his almost black hair, on down his lean, broad-shouldered body. He wore a tuxedo comfortably, not looking as if he wished he were at home in sweats.

"Like you, art is personal to me, Miss Chandler. Although certainly some pieces have shocked my friends." They wandered to the next painting. "This one, for example. What do you think of it?"

Unlike the other portraits, this piece had an almost photographic feel to it, the sepia tones warm but the image stark. A bridal gown lay jumbled on the floor beside the woman portrayed. Tulle from her veil wound around her feet. Otherwise she was nude, her arms drawn across her body in a classic pose to hide her womanliness, the bouquet she carried startling against her pale abdomen. Her eyes were downcast. A lone tear trailed her cheek.

The untitled painting bothered Cristina in ways she'd have to think about later. Her initial reaction was simple, however, and she offered it to the still, silent man beside her. "I think a bride should look more like the woman in the first portrait. This woman's not in love."

"My impression as well. It is De La Hoya's newest work, I understand."

"I wonder why he didn't title it. It seems obvious to me… *Sacrifice*," she said.

He angled his head toward her. She felt a heat from his gaze that seared her all the way through.

"Why do you call it that?" he asked.

"There's something old-worldly about it. About all of De La Hoya's work. In this one I see a woman of another century, one who didn't choose her groom, but was chosen."

"An obedient woman."

"But only to a degree." Cristina gestured at the painting wineglass. "It's there, in her posture—that little bit she may not have choices, but she still has free-

gain her?"

friends?"

The hushed intensity of his voice made her hesitate. Something about the man hypnotized. Enticed. Lured.

"Self-satisfaction, Mr. Marquez. No one can take her soul."

"Unless she weakens."

Cristina didn't know what to make of him. He was a cool one. And intelligent. And still she sensed he was not quite civilized. Dangerous. Yes, the word suited him. Temptingly dangerous, unlike any other man she'd known.

"What a strange conversation," she said, forcing a smile. "How did we even start it?"

"Because I watched you—"

Sparks ignited in her body as she waited for him to finish the sentence. Why in the world was a man like him interested in her? She couldn't fathom why he had picked her out of the crowd.

"I watched the way you studied the work," he said finally. "You have a critical eye. A discerning one. Your friend, for example, reacted emotionally to the paintings."

"So did I."

"Yes. But you study *why* it affects you. You have an artist's heart."

It wasn't a line. She didn't know why she knew that, but she was sure of it. Another man might have used the same words, and she would have scoffed at them—and walked away. This wasn't a man given to idle flattery.

Still, why had he singled her out? She usually attracted the intellectual types, or the needy ones. Not intense, attractive, dangerous men who made her wish she was a different kind of woman altogether. A prettier woman. A sexier woman.

No, men weren't drawn to her because their hormones jumped when they were around her. They were drawn to her because—

"Look who I found!"

Jen's cheerful announcement seemed an abomination in the rarefied air of the Galeria Secreto. To make matters worse, Jen had Jason Grimes in tow. Jason, who had become her shadow. Jason, who had suddenly become her father's favor conversation. She suspected she knew the reason why, but she intended to ignore it for as long as possible.

"If you'd told me you were coming tonight, Cris, I would have escorted you," Jason said.

If I'd wanted to be escorted, I would have called you, Cristina thought, too polite to say the words in public. Especially not with *him* standing there, listening, watching. "I didn't think you cared much about art," she said before introducing the men.

"If you will excuse me." Gabriel Marquez nodded his apologies, then left.

Cristina tried not to watch him go. Genuinely tried. But the pull was magnetic, and she didn't seem to have any control over it.

"Who was that?" Jason asked.

"I've never met him before. We were discussing the portraits."

Jason looked around. "Some good stuff here. Sexy."

There was a difference between sexy and sexual, but she knew Jason wouldn't be interested in discussing nuance and subtlety when all he saw was a nude female body. She looked past him. Mr. Marquez stopped to talk with an elegant middle-aged woman. He held her hand; his thumb brushed her skin. Goose bumps rose on Cristina's flesh. Warmth spiraled in her hand.

The woman smiled at him, then pouted, then flirted, using her eyes like invitations. Oh, please don't let me have looked at him like that, Cristina prayed.

Gabe watched her with Jason Grimes. He'd detected no sign of recognition from Grimes at their introduction, had seen nothing in the younger man's aristocratic features except jeal- ... then dismissal. If Grimes happened to mention meeting ... his father, the repercussions could be fascinating, in- ... ost wished for it to happen.

... h and water, he shifted his gaze to observe ... larly pleased with her familiarity with ... her as they discussed a painting.

She was much different from what he'd anticipated from the photo, which obviously hadn't been taken recently. For one thing, she'd gained weight. And not just a few pounds. She looked softer, more approachable, less brittle, not the cool, sleek woman of privilege he'd expected. More than that, there was a lushness to her that made him think of rumpled sheets and a morning sun—which made his task not only easier but something he looked forward to.

Her generous curves were clothed in a sapphire blue dress that was simple and elegant, and perfect for her—high-necked and sleeveless, fitted at the waist, hugging her hips. Her hair shimmered like fire, a shade somewhere between gold and red, and had the slightest curl to the thick fullness that fell over her shoulders. Her eyes were blue, as he'd guessed, but flecked with gold and…innocence.

Innocence held no appeal for him, either in body or spirit.

He would have the gallery manager, Raymond, photograph her tonight, unobtrusively, from several angles.

He started to take another sip, then stopped, the glass an inch from his lips as he considered everything he knew about her. The irony didn't escape him—Cristina Chandler would be perfect for Sebastian.

Gabe toasted the air. *Sorry, old friend.* He swallowed the contents of the glass and grimaced, diverting his thoughts.

The secret to knowing who this woman was and how useful she might be was somehow connected to why she'd gained weight. Or perhaps when the earlier photo was taken she'd lost weight. Whichever had occurred, there was a reason, as well as a reason for why she'd moved out of the family home and into her own apartment in San Francisco. And why she could afford to do so when her father was in debt to his earlobes. All these issues should be addressed before he took the next step.

He focused on her once more as she examined another canvas, the most traditional portrait of the showing, and yet she seemed to see something beneath the surface, something that held her attention much longer than it had her friends', who had both moved on. She pressed her wineglass to her lips, dragged it across them, touched the tip of her tongue just below the rim, like a lover's caress.

She turned then and caught him staring. He didn't look away. He knew how to court a woman, how to flatter, how to seduce. The only women he respected were the ones who turned him down. If that said something deplorable about him, so be it. Respect wasn't necessary for a satisfactory liaison, not for the routinely brief duration of his relationships, anyway.

She looked away first. He went in search of Raymond.

Two

Two days later Gabe watched from his vantage point inside the Galeria Secreto as Cristina walked up the street. For the unusually warm fall weather, she wore a simple long skirt and low-necked T-shirt in the same shade of lavender, but relieved by a flashy necklace of multicolored, sparkly glass beads.

A tinkling bell announced her as she breezed through the front door and headed for Raymond's desk. Gabe scarcely breathed, not wanting to alert her to his presence.

He didn't have answers to all of his questions yet—and he shouldn't proceed until he did—but he didn't have the luxury of unlimited time, either. Although there could be a certain satisfaction in disrupting their engagement after the fact, too, he didn't want to wait that long.

The answers would have to come from the source, not from Doc's skill with people and computers.

"Miss Chandler," Raymond said effusively, hurrying into the room. "Thank you so much for coming."

"You said it was important."

"Yes. Please be seated." He also sat and folded his hands

on the desk. "I regret to tell you that Mr. De La Hoya has chosen not to accept your father's commission."

"I appreciate your letting me know," she said, "but shouldn't you be calling my father? He's the one who made the inquiry."

"That would be my doing," Gabe said, moving into range. "I asked Raymond to arrange this meeting."

Cristina looked up at Gabriel Marquez, wondering how long he'd been within earshot. Since she arrived? Probably. He moved like a panther stalking its prey. She should be angry. She knew she should. But excitement tipped the scale of should and shouldn't. Her stomach filled with a huge quantity of tiny butterflies, flitting and landing, flitting and landing.

Raymond removed himself quietly from the room.

"Miss Chandler," Gabe said, his gaze direct.

"Mr. Marquez."

"Forgive me for resorting to subterfuge. I didn't know if you would be open to my calling you on this matter. I thought perhaps a neutral meeting place…"

"To discuss what?" She watched him half sit on the corner of Raymond's desk. He wore light linen slacks and a burgundy polo shirt, but nothing else about him seemed casual.

"I overheard your conversation the other night when you and your friend were discussing the portrait your father wants. It was rude of me, of course. I apologize."

"Do you? A genuine apology or one you think is required?"

He smiled. "Ah, a cynic. I'm surprised."

"A skeptic," she corrected. "I do recognize a man with an agenda."

His smile deepened. "One that coincides with yours, I believe. I have a solution to your dilemma."

Cristina forced herself to relax. She settled into the chair and crossed her legs. "I'm not the least upset about De La Hoya's decision not to paint me," she said, although it wasn't entirely true. She wondered why, all right, even as a quilt of relief had settled over her at the news. "I really don't have a dilemma to solve."

"You would like to pacify your father, wouldn't you?"

She looked away from him. Damn it. Of course she would. How had he figured that out in such a short time? "My father will survive the slap to his ego."

"How old is he, Miss Chandler?"

"Call me Cristina," she said, stalling, comprehending his point at once but irritated that he used the ammunition. "Eighty-two."

"In good health?"

"As healthy as eighty-two can be, Mr. Marquez."

"Gabe." He smiled slightly. "What if there were a way to provide your father with a portrait he believes is De La Hoya but at a cost much less than he charges?"

"I'd be interested in hearing the details."

He lifted a leather binder from atop the desk and passed it to her. "I think you'll agree that the paintings photographed there are of a style resembling De La Hoya's."

Cristina examined them critically. "These are landscapes, not people, which are two entirely different skills artistically. But I'll grant that otherwise there are similarities in style. Certainly the artist has captured the same general mood and texture and tone."

"What if that artist were to do your portrait—and do it well? Do you think your father would know the difference?"

"It wouldn't matter, because I would. Surely the artist couldn't sign his own name. My father would know by the signature, if nothing else."

"If we somehow found a way around that problem?"

"That's a big *if.*" Cristina closed the folder. She flattened her hands on the cover, curved her fingers over the edge. "Why does it matter to you?"

"Because I want very much to paint you."

Cristina sucked in a breath. Oh, my. She was flattered, and appalled, and far too tempted. And she had a very hard time believing—

"You doubt me," he said, taking her hand in his, watching her.

She glanced at the album again. Knowing now that he was

the artist, she was tempted to take a second look. Composure. She had to dig deep for it.

"We have a kinship, don't you agree? You've felt it, as have I," he said, brushing his thumb over her knuckles. "A connection between artist and subject improves the finished product."

She was reminded of how he'd rubbed his thumb along the woman's hand the other night. So, the gesture probably meant nothing to him but a means of turning off a woman's brain while she pondered his incredible physique, his utter maleness, and his you-are-the-only-woman-for-me eyes.

"I'll amend the offer, then," he said as she remained silent. "I will charge you nothing, and you may do with the painting what you will. You can't lose, Cristina."

Oh, Lord, she loved the way he said her name. No one had ever said her name like that before. Not with an accent, but with a sultry edge, a tempting—

She stood and walked away from him, trying to find a way to elevate the discussion, trying to leave attraction—no, *lust*—out of it. She wasn't a teenager. She wasn't even frustrated. Well, not *that* frustrated. So, she hadn't had sex since— She didn't want to think about how long it had been, and it hadn't been wonderful, then, anyway. With this man, however—

Stop, stop, stop. You don't know anything about him.

Except that he had her hormones dancing pirouettes on every cell of her body, charging her with energy, as if she could light up the Golden Gate Bridge just by touching the steel.

"Say yes," he said quietly.

He'd come up behind her, was standing so close she could feel his body heat all the way to her ankles. She wanted to lean against him. She wanted him to put his arms around her, nuzzle her neck, tell her she was beautiful. What was happening to her? *She didn't know the man.*

Gabe lifted a hand toward her shoulder, then let it fall. He knew he affected her. Her breath came short and shallow. Her perfume became more potent as her body temperature rose.

"Do you need recommendations of my character?" he asked, backing away.

"That would help." She turned to face him.

"Inspector Leslie O'Keefe with the San Francisco P.D. would vouch for me. Raymond, of course. Plenty of others, if necessary."

"Are you a professional artist?"

"Do I make my living from it? No. But I'm serious about it."

"What kind of business are you in?"

"More businesses than I can count. All of them legitimate," he added, one corner of his mouth curving upward. "I'm a venture capitalist."

"You make money from investments?"

"Sometimes. Sometimes I lose money. It's the challenge that appeals to me, and the work fills up most of my life. Painting relaxes me."

"What's your connection to this gallery?"

"I own it."

He waited as she sifted the information. "Say yes," he urged again when the silence dragged on.

Cristina considered all the angles. It was exhausting pretending to be so sophisticated for this urbane, mysterious man. She felt like a mouse trapped in his maze. And she had the feeling that he could drop mirrors along the path anytime he chose.

He couldn't be much more than five years older than she, yet he seemed to have lived a lifetime longer. Being alone with him for hours at a time would be a challenge. He tempted her in ways she'd never been tempted before, was unwillingly flattered by his intense and direct gaze.

But temptation and flattery aside, she knew she could also use the time to her advantage, helping to cool Jason's recent, bewildering attention and her father's sudden preoccupation with her getting married.

Oh, she knew what was expected of her. Father thought he'd been subtle, but she read him well. He wanted her to marry Jason. He was in dire need of money, and the marriage would somehow help. He would be angry with her if she ignored her responsibilities for long.

It was a risk she was willing to take, because she'd never felt this pull toward anyone or anything in her life. And she wanted to experience it to the fullest. The problem with Jason would be there when Gabe was part of her past—if it mattered by then.

She finally looked at him, admiring his ability to wait her out. His patience appealed to her, showing her a level of maturity she was unused to from the men of her acquaintance.

"When would you like to start?" she asked.

"As soon as possible. I can adjust my schedule to yours."

"I work at home, therefore I set my own hours. I imagine you want daylight, natural light." At his nod, she picked up her purse from the chair and tugged the strap over her shoulder. "Name the time."

He extracted a business card from a slim gold case and passed it to her. "I also work at home. Eleven tomorrow morning?"

"Fine." She glanced at the card. His address put him smack in the middle of Pacific Heights, an area filled with wonderful Victorian-design houses that were huge, old and expensive. It was a world she came from, but had never felt comfortable in. "Please tell Raymond that if my father contacts him about the portrait, he should just stall for a while. Father won't like it, but he thinks he understands the artistic temperament."

"Why does he?"

She smiled. "Because of me. I'll see you tomorrow."

"I'm fine," Cristina said into the phone, wandering around her apartment as she spoke to her father. She hadn't accomplished anything since she'd left the gallery, and three projects awaited her attention. She'd gotten in the last word with Gabe, which pleased her, but the anticipation had rendered her useless otherwise. "And, no, I haven't seen a single hoodlum, Father. It's very quiet."

"There was no reason to move out. You had your own wing, for heaven's sake."

"It's not the same as having a place of my own. It was time for me to spread my wings. We've discussed this again and again."

"Yes, I know. I've been smothering you since your mother died. You'll have a place of your own when you marry."

"No, I won't. I'll have my husband's place."

He sighed. "I don't understand the modern woman. Your mother was content to join me in my life and make it her own."

"I'm not her, Father."

"As you remind me so often. I must go now, my dear. Oh, by the way, I gave Jason your new address and phone number. I expect he'll check in."

He hung up before she could utter a word of protest. Logically she knew she couldn't keep her location a secret from Jason, but she resented her father being the one to tell him.

When someone knocked on her door, she knew without question who would be there. He'd probably been sitting in his car with his cellular phone, waiting for her father to call him, so she couldn't pretend to be gone.

She didn't want him in her apartment, in her space. She'd divorced herself from that life, and Jason would bring it back with him.

With a sigh, she opened the door and invited him in, unwillingly comparing Jason to Gabriel Marquez. They were close to the same height and weight, although their builds were entirely different, Gabe appearing more powerful, in physique and sheer presence. Where Gabe was dark, Jason was light. Most significantly, Jason wasn't the slightest bit exciting or intriguing or…dangerous. She watched him glance around the room that combined a living room, bedroom and kitchen. The furnishings were few, but they were hers.

"You *like* it here, Cris?"

She counted to five. "I love it. Why wouldn't I?"

"It's so small."

"It suits me. So, what's going on?"

"I have tickets to the opera. Friday night."

"You hate the opera."

"Yeah." He jammed his hands in his front pockets. "But you don't. I want to take you."

She studied him for a moment. "Have a seat."

They sat on the sofa, the only piece of furniture she owned other than her bed and computer desk. "What's this all about, Jason? We've known each other almost forever. This is totally unlike you, asking me for a date."

"I've been through a lot lately. You know. My life is different now."

"Because of the scandal? But that's your father's problem. It's his building that collapsed. His name was all over the headlines, not yours. And it's his reputation that's in question."

"You don't think I'm affected by the fallout? Don't be naive, Cris. Until we find that guy who was paralyzed in the accident and prove he's the one who caused it, I'm invisible. People don't return my calls. I get the cold shoulder at the club. I have become persona non grata. You are the only one who didn't turn away."

If he only knew how little thought she'd given the whole mess. She'd been too wrapped up with planning her move to her own apartment to think about anyone else. Maybe she did owe him something. He'd always been nice to her, even when their parents weren't around. His family had bought a house near hers when she was five, but Richard Grimes's wealth was too new, and it had taken years for him to earn minimal acceptance in local society. The scandal had become a convenient excuse to ignore him.

Cristina swallowed a sigh, remembering how Jason had volunteered to escort her to her senior prom—her only invitation for the event. She'd been painfully shy then. Even now, she had to force herself to be more outgoing when she'd rather stand back and observe.

She looked at him. They were both going through changes that had taken them out of the social hub they'd always known—although hers was by choice. She didn't want to encourage him, not when something new and exciting awaited her, but she couldn't find it in her heart to turn away from him, either.

She touched the back of his hand. "Of course I'll go with you. Thank you for thinking of me."

"Really? I'll pick you up at seven-thirty. We'll have a late supper after."

"Fine." She followed him to the front door, startled by how fast he was leaving. Apparently he'd gotten what he came for, and that was that. No idle chitchat for this man. If he really thought that just being seen with her would help, well, she could make that sacrifice.

He clasped her hand and shook it, then he leaned back through the doorway and kissed her, right on the lips. On a scale from one to ten, she gave him a one in both technique and excitement level. She resisted wiping the back of her hand across her mouth when he pulled away.

"Bye," he called as he hurried out to the street.

Cristina shut the door, then went into the kitchen to get something to wash away the experience. She drank half a glass of iced tea before she came up for air.

The planets must be out of alignment or something, she decided. All of a sudden she'd become some sort of femme fatale, a whole new role for her. Two men had taken a more-than-average interest in her. One might as well be her brother—she'd certainly never looked at him as anything other than a platonic friend. The second man she couldn't even begin to define. But she had a hard time believing that she was the kind of woman who normally drew Gabriel Marquez's attention.

So, it appeared that both men had agendas and neither of them were sharing the itemized list with her, leaving her in a quandary. The biggest adventure of her life was about to begin, and she wasn't sure what to pack for the journey.

Three

―――

Right on time. From his office window, Gabe watched Cristina exit the taxicab. Not surprised at her punctuality, he left the room, then waited on the landing as his part-time housekeeper directed her up the stairs.

He watched her trail her hand along the mahogany banister, her fingertips caressing the polished wood. He saw her focus on the individual paintings hung at precise intervals on the wall along the staircase, the same scene but depicted at different times of year and in different weather. Light and shadows changed with the seasons, creating individual moods.

"Good morning," she said as she reached the landing and accepted his outstretched hand. "What a beautiful home, and what incredible work you do."

"We have to go up one more flight to the studio." He curved his fingers around hers. "And you don't have to flatter me, but I thank you."

"Now, you strike me as a man with a firm grip on his ego." She smiled, casting him a sideways glance as they climbed the next staircase. "My opinion of your work probably doesn't even matter to you."

He noted the teasing light in her eyes. "Even a secure ego needs feeding."

She made a sound of agreement. "Have you lived here long?"

"A few years."

"So your risks pay off more often than not."

He released her hand as they stepped into the garret room he'd turned into a studio. "I don't seem to run out of beer and pretzels."

"I'll bet. Oh! Oh, Gabe, this is wonderful!"

His time in the studio was limited, but he enjoyed every second. Skylights allowed the sun to flood the space. Windows replaced the front and back walls. Although called a garret, it was really too large and airy for the title, thanks to the changes he'd made. He'd spent the morning straightening up the room. Usually he didn't bother. It was the only area of his life he didn't keep filed, sorted, computerized or pigeonholed.

He watched her move to the back window, which overlooked his garden, her teal-colored skirt undulating around her calves as she walked, a contrast to her demure sleeveless blouse printed with tiny flowers and buttoned to her throat. On her feet lilac-painted toenails drew attention to her strappy sandals. Gold bracelets danced along her left wrist, tinkling sweetly. She didn't wear a watch, which pleased him. She wasn't in a hurry.

"Beautiful," she said, turning to him.

"I can't take credit for it. I only enjoy someone else's hard work."

"But beauty and color are important to you. You surround yourself with it. That's obvious in your work."

"And my subject." He waited to see if she blushed. She didn't, but her posture changed, as if she didn't believe him. "I'll just be sketching you today, Cristina, and conversing. I need to know more about you before we talk about clothing and tone."

"My father will want something appropriate to hang with

the other generations in the family gallery.'' She paused. ''That sounds really pretentious, doesn't it? Again.''

''Traditions die hard. Please, come sit here and let me study you.''

Cristina moved to the appointed chair he'd placed directly under a skylight. Her heart hadn't stopped thumping since she'd stepped into his house. Her body was warm and her temperature still climbing. She'd intentionally worn something nondescript because...because— She didn't know why, for sure. Only that she needed some kind of armor for now.

If De La Hoya had actually taken the commission, she would have allowed him—because he undoubtedly would have demanded—artistic control. Except that she certainly wouldn't have posed nude.

Maybe he'd turned down the commission because he'd deduced that what her father wanted would be too traditional for his interest. She'd never know, of course, since his reclusive life meant that they would never cross paths.

''What are you thinking about?'' Gabe asked.

Startled out of her thoughts, she fidgeted. ''Alejandro De La Hoya.''

''Well. I'm flattered.''

She smiled. ''I was uncomfortable having you study me. I had to think about something else. Have you ever met him?''

He made a noncommittal sound as he pulled up a rolling stool beside her and hefted a sketch pad into his lap. ''What kind of music do you like?''

''Classical. Opera, in particular. Most especially Verdi. I'm going to see *Rigoletto* tomorrow night with Jason Grimes. He's the man you met the other night.''

''Yes, I remember him.''

She listened to the sound of his pencil as he sketched— short, quick strokes detailing her face in profile. She was glad she didn't have to see him eye her inch by inch. ''How about you? What's your music of choice?''

''Wagner. Miles Davis. Segovia.''

''Eclectic taste,'' she commented, tempted to look in his

direction. There was tension in his voice that hadn't been there before. "Why don't you put on some music now?"

"Because I don't like it to influence me in the early stages. I figure out what suits the subject, then I choose the music to accompany me while I work. Your hair needs to be pulled back from your face."

He set down his pad and pencil, then walked to a nearby chest of drawers. In a minute he returned, a length of black ribbon in his hand. He moved behind her.

"I'll do it," he said as she started to gather her hair into a ponytail.

She closed her eyes. He combed her hair with his fingers as he pulled it back. The cool satin of the ribbon glided across her neck. His fingertips grazed her skin. She shivered. She wasn't used to familiarity, especially from a stranger.

A man.

She'd grown up in a house where people seldom touched. Oh, she'd felt loved, but physical warmth was missing. Sometimes when she'd stayed overnight with friends, she'd seen how different families could be. On the other hand, no one argued at her house, which was also good. She froze during arguments. Logic slipped away, leaving only the emotion she was feeling, and she could never convey her emotions clearly while under duress.

"One of the first things I noticed about you," Gabe said from behind her, "was your hair. More beautiful than fire."

"I was born in the wrong century." She tried to shrug off the mesmerizing lure of his voice. "I figured Titian would have hired me to model," she said, referring to the Renaissance painter whose use of color brought him acclaim, particularly his redheaded subjects.

"Your hair is more gold than red." Gabe moved then, coming to a stop in front of her, staring at her long enough to make her squirm. "Had Rubens gotten a look at you, however— Ah, I've made you uncomfortable. Forgive me. I tend to analyze too much."

Cristina didn't know whether to be flattered or insulted. One of Rubens's claims to fame was his paintings of voluptuous women. How many times in her adult life had she wished she'd lived in Rubens's time instead of now?

"I used to be a lot thinner," she said, then clamped her mouth shut.

"Oh?" Gabe settled in the seat beside her again and started sketching, pleased to be pulling information from her so easily. "Was thinner better, Cristina? Did you like yourself more?"

"No." She blew out a breath, relaxing. "No. If anything, I hated it."

He wanted tension back in her face. It would make for a much more interesting portrait than soft and sweet. He could tell her that she was beautiful. That would surely bring back the tension. Some women thrived on flattery, whether true or false. But not this woman. Even her posture had indicated it earlier. "Why did you hate it?"

"It wasn't me. It wasn't real."

"Had you been ill?"

"No."

She looked at her lap, and he stopped sketching to wait.

"I was a surprise, mid-life baby," she said finally. "I came along twenty-five years into my parents' marriage, when my mother was forty-six and my father fifty-five, long after they'd given up hope of ever having a child. They didn't quite know what to do with me."

Again, he waited. After a minute he rolled his stool directly in front of her and set his sketch pad aside. He clasped her hands. She looked up. His gaze never strayed from hers. "Tell me."

She swallowed. "They had certain expectations."

"Unrealistic ones."

Cristina nodded. "My father was a state senator, so we lived in a fishbowl. I was to be well mannered, and studious, and a dainty little lady. The well-mannered part I could manage. And when my mother became terminally ill, I tried to make myself into what she wanted—a dainty woman. It was the hardest thing I'd done, but before she died two years ago, I'd made her proud, and I'm glad I did. I learned a lot about myself because of it.'' She squeezed his hands. ''Why am I telling you this?''

''Because you want me to paint the real Cristina.''

God. He was right! He was absolutely right. ''Weight and all,'' she said.

''You. As you. You're lovely.''

She shook her head.

''Yes.'' He lifted a hand to her face, stroked the flesh along her cheekbone with his thumb. ''You weren't born in the wrong century, either. I will paint you not only as you want the future Chandler generations to see you, but as *I* see you. Then you'll know how beautiful you are.''

Oh, he tempted her with his words. He wanted to paint some exotic, erotic woman that wasn't the least like her, maybe even a second, more-personal portrait in the De La Hoya style. And the allure of giving in to the flattery was strong, even as she knew it wasn't something she would ever feel comfortable doing. What if the painting ended up in some gallery where someone she knew saw it? What if someone told her father? She'd disappointed him enough lately.

And the biggest ''what if'' of all—what if when Gabe saw her unclothed, he was repulsed. His imagination had undoubtedly painted a better picture than reality.

''I think we should focus on the portrait that will please my father,'' she said, aware of changes in her body. Her nipples had drawn taut the moment he'd touched her face and now pulsed with a gentle ache.

She wondered whether he kissed hard or soft, whether he enticed or attacked, whether he would know how inexperienced she was. Jason's kiss had been one hard, closed mouth pressed to another. She'd bet her trust fund that Gabriel Marquez never kissed with a closed mouth, nor hurried out the door the next second.

Cold seeped into her when he moved back, then she warmed as his gaze dropped to her breasts and he took note of her reaction to him. Confused, she stood and walked to the front window. ''I'm not too sure that this is a good idea.''

"On the contrary, Cristina. This is the best idea I've ever had. I hope I can convince you of the same thing."

"Let's change the subject."

A few seconds of silence filled the room. From outside she heard a bird trill, a car drive past, a child shriek with laughter. Uncomfortable with the quiet inside, she started to turn.

"Don't move."

The sound of pencil on paper held her suspended. She could see him in her peripheral vision, could feel the intensity of his focus.

"Put your right hand on the window, level with your shoulder. Spread your fingers open," he instructed her. "Tip your head back a little. Look as far into the horizon as you can. Shoulders back. Good."

He worked in silence for several minutes. "Put your left hand to your chest, over your heart. A bit lower. No—"

Gabe moved closer, then placed her hand where he wanted, spreading her fingers apart like her other hand, not letting his fingers brush her breasts.

A wistful pose, Gabe thought. "Angle toward me a little." He flipped a page. "Now, turn only your head and look directly at me." The pencil glided. "Who are you right now?"

A long pause, then, "Someone from a previous life."

"Tell me."

"A...a New England sea captain's wife, I think, watching for my husband's ship to return after a long journey."

"A woman who waits."

"A woman who worries. And pines."

"Do you love your husband?" he asked.

"Oh, yes."

"How long have you been married?"

A faraway look settled in her eyes.

"Ten years. He's home only half the year. I worry about him."

"Do you have children?"

"No. It's my one sorrow."

"How do you feel when you see his ship come into port?"

She smiled. "Thrilled. Grateful. Relieved."

"Do you wait at home for him or go to the ship?"

"He's too busy to see me for a while. I take a bath, dress in something feminine, make sure there's something to eat. For afterward," she added. "He's hungry for me first."

"When he comes through your front door, what happens?" He flipped another page. The clean sheet would capture a new impression.

"I fly into his arms. He whirls me around and around. I press my nose against his neck and he smells wonderful. Like him. Like no one else in the world. Then he kisses me, and the long, lonely months melt away. He carries me upstairs."

Gabe watched the changes in her expressions. She had become the fictitious captain's wife. Her imagination had taken her away and planted her firmly in the scene. Her muscles were tense, her body taut. Her nipples pressed at the fabric covering them.

He tamped down his own reaction, one that shocked the hell out of him. He'd thought himself immune to innocence, to purity, to sweetness. He much preferred an equal partner, one who led, who took, who demanded. He didn't think that defined Cristina.

Seeing her start to relax, he began sketching and questioning again. "Are you faithful while he's gone?"

"Absolutely."

"He's a good lover." A statement, not a question.

"Beyond good," Cristina said, a smile forming.

"Why? What makes him special?"

"It's not what he does. It's why he does it."

"Why?"

"He loves me."

Dead silence. His pencil skidded, seemed to dig a hole in the paper. Cristina watched his focus shift as he absorbed her words. She was enjoying his game, which tempted her, dared her, excited her—more than any man had done with actions. Part of his allure was the danger, she knew.

"What he does is also important," he said.

She moved a shoulder. "Maybe. More important is how I feel afterward."

He continued to sketch, his thoughts well hidden.

"You want to comment," she said. "What's stopping you?"

He hesitated. "You might change your mind about posing."

"You've demanded honesty from me. You've managed to pry some of my secrets loose from moorings I didn't think anyone could. Don't deny me the same insight into what drives you."

"Men view sex differently. Women like to fantasize that it's different when she's the right woman for him. It's not true. It still comes down to physical satisfaction for men, not emotional."

"Always?"

"I suppose I can't speak for all men. We don't discuss the point as women do. But I believe it's so."

She rolled her head, easing kinks settling in her neck, feeling sorry for him because he was so disillusioned about love.

"Tired?" he asked.

"A little."

"Let's stop for now. I'll order lunch."

He watched her shift her shoulders as he asked his housekeeper to serve lunch on the screened porch facing the garden. He hung up the phone just as Cristina put her hand on a stack of paintings leaning against a wall.

"May I?" she asked.

He had a decision to make, quickly. After a minute, he nodded. Then he waited.

At first she simply seemed caught up in the images she was examining, then something changed. She slowed down. Concentrated. Focused. She turned toward him, accusation in her eyes.

"These paintings are signed Marquez. But the style... It's so distinctive. I couldn't see it in the photographs. You're— You're not—"

"I am Gabriel Alejandro De La Hoya y Marquez." *And I am descended from kings.*

The tag came automatically to mind, an old game he and his mother had played. She'd always made him say the whole thing together. He'd stopped when he was fifteen and knew better.

"I don't understand," she said, looking around. "There's no curtain. No two-way mirror. There's just—"

"Me and you. The ridiculous rumor is just that, Cristina, started by someone who thought it would be diverting to say that is the way De La Hoya works. It's part of the mystique."

"Why?"

"Why the secrecy? Because it places a higher value on the work."

"And you're only interested in making money."

He watched her expression close up. He'd disappointed her. "I make a very comfortable living. I don't need what I get from my art, but I enjoy the game, one I have to play out now because I'm too far into it to stop. But that doesn't mean I don't love it. I do. I also love the challenge of taking a losing company and making it successful. Or helping a determined immigrant start a business. Or endowing an artist. Painting feeds my soul. It also puts food on the plate of some starving artist, giving him or her the freedom to pursue their dreams full-time."

They faced each other like duelists in the streets of the Old West. Cristina intentionally moved toward him, needing some kind of action, some forward momentum. The shock had immobilized her. "And you've already decided that I'm worthy of your trust. You don't think I'd tell anyone the truth," she said, studying his expression.

"I know it for a fact. We have a connection. That connection is only going to get stronger by your knowing the truth. Alejandro De La Hoya is a known quantity. Gabriel Marquez is not. Not as an artist, anyway. I want you to have confidence in me to do what's right for you in this portrait. I think you would trust De La Hoya more than Marquez."

"Well, you're wrong." She stopped in front of him. "I don't think it will make a difference, except that I like knowing the truth. Your secret is safe with me."

"I know."

She smiled. "You were the tiniest bit worried, though, weren't you? I could see it in your eyes."

"It's always a leap of faith."

"I knew there was something you were keeping hidden."

"Did you?"

She liked the arrogant lift of his brow. He was a complicated man who had just made himself more so, therefore more intriguing, and more dangerous. She would have to open up to him now in ways she hadn't anticipated.

"Tell me, Gabe— Is that what I call you?"

He nodded.

"Tell me. Do you have affairs with your subjects? Jen was sure by looking at the paintings that you do."

"Is that what you're looking for?"

"I asked you first."

He hesitated. "I choose my subjects carefully. Sometimes I've chosen to paint someone I'm involved with. Usually, it isn't the case. Certainly the older I've gotten, the less the two mesh."

"Thank you for your honesty."

Gabe reached behind her and loosened the ribbon, pulling it slowly across her neck. "Now you must answer my question."

She pressed a shaky hand to his chest. "If my father had his way, I'd be engaged to Jason Grimes today and married to him next week."

"Which tells me nothing. Certainly it doesn't answer my question. Are you looking to have an affair?"

She shifted her weight. "No."

Her hesitation gave him a different answer, but he wouldn't call her on it. Not yet. "All right."

He found it endearing, the way surprise and disappointment washed across her face before she stepped back. What an innocent she was. If her father played the right cards—the emotional ones—she'd marry Jason Grimes. For her father's sake, of course, not hers. She believed in love—or the fantasy of love. But she also believed in family. Losing weight to please her dying mother said it all.

Gabe loved his mother. She'd been the only constant in his life. But he had never allowed her to tell him how to live his life—

Except once. He had promised her he wouldn't exact revenge against his father, worthless bastard that he was, even though the opportunity and means had been within Gabe's reach many times. What was the purpose of having money and the power that came with it if he couldn't use it as he wished?

In that sense he supposed he was like Arthur Chandler or Richard Grimes. Grimes would use his wealth to buy back lost power. Gabe would do the same thing, if necessary. The difference was that he would never get in the same kind of trouble—and expect his son to bail him out.

But the ultimate sacrificial lamb was Cristina Chandler. And lamb she was, one in need of protection. Her powerful but desperate father had turned her into a commodity, her value set according to how well she could get him out of a jam.

Then again, Gabe seemed to be doing the same thing.

"You've drifted to another time zone," she commented.

"I was thinking I should paint you beneath a bower of ivy."

"With flowers?"

"You are colorful enough on your own. Your dress should be white, even. Something outwardly virtuous."

She raised her brows. "Outwardly?"

"At first glance you would seem the very essence of innocence, then when the viewer focuses on your face, there'll be something different. The hidden depths, not so hidden."

"My father won't see it."

"It doesn't matter. You and I will see. And understand." He watched her pluck a purple mum from an arrangement on the chest. She snapped the stem a little shorter and tucked the bloom into her hair, over her ear.

"Do you have a dress that would be right?" he asked.

"Nothing remotely close."

He nodded. "We will go shopping."

Cristina sent an army of control to quell her rioting nerves. She'd been edgy when she arrived, had gotten edgier since then. Now, pinpricks of panic stabbed at her. "I'm capable of choosing a dress myself."

"If you're worried about me seeing what size dress you wear…"

She stiffened. What was he, psychic? A mind reader? She couldn't go through with this, after all. He was burrowing deep inside her, this man who saw beyond what anyone else had ever seen. It scared her, excited her, baffled her. And it made her acknowledge feelings she'd never had before. She hadn't lied to him, not consciously. She didn't want an affair. She just didn't know what she was going to do with these physical cravings and sexual yearnings, however.

"You're not going to have any secrets from me when we're done," he finished.

"None?"

He shook his head. "In designer clothes, you wear a four-teen. Off the rack, a sixteen. I don't give a damn. Neither should you. You told me yourself that you hated being thinner."

How did he *do* that? He knew way too much about women. Yellow warning flags went up all around her. She ignored them. "But I also hate having you know what size I wear. I may have come to some acceptance of myself along the way, but you're a man, after all. An attractive man."

"A man who's telling you this truth, Cristina. I think you're beautiful just as you are. And this is the last time we are discussing this." He touched the flower in her hair. "Relax with me. Be yourself. Be playful when you feel like it. Sensual when you feel like it. Angry, even. Be you. You know that's what you want more than anything. Trust me."

"My mother told me never to trust a man who said, 'Trust me.'"

"She sounds like a wise woman."

"I miss her."

The simplicity of her words made his gut clench. There were many levels of loneliness. He'd known a lot of them himself. But he'd chosen his life, chosen to be alone most of the time, to stay out of the limelight. The only person he'd ever missed was Sebastian, who'd done nothing to harm any-one in his entire life. Sebastian, who'd insisted on forging a friendship between four completely opposite boys and one girl. A friendship that had endured for eighteen years but was floundering now without the bond that Sebastian provided.

Sebastian had watched Gabe track Richard Grimes's every move through the years and understood Gabe's deep hatred of the man. More important, Sebastian had taken it upon himself to try to expose Grimes's unscrupulous business dealings. Gabe should have trusted his instincts and not allowed Sebastian to make himself the bait. Now he was struggling to walk again—and fighting for his reputation as well.

"Gabe?"

He breathed again. "Yes?"

"You keep disappearing on me."

He lifted her hand to his lips, felt her retreat at first, then relax. "After lunch we'll do a little shopping, shall we, Miss Chandler?"

Cristina held her breath. Inhibitions fled her body faster than she could count to ten. He was offering her a freedom she'd never known. Suddenly, she felt safe. Very, very safe. He was going to demand a lot of her, but he wouldn't hurt her. If she got hurt, it would be her own fault. This wasn't a man looking for commitment. She understood that.

She wished he would kiss her mouth. She waited a few seconds, hoping he'd take the hint, or read her mind, or what-ever he did to figure her out so well. But he just waited, the patience she'd seen in him from the beginning settling around them.

Plus, she'd said no, after all. She supposed she should re-spect him for taking her seriously.

"You can't act like my lord and master while we shop."

He smiled. "I promise."

"No leaning back in a chair and scrutinizing each dress. No twirling your finger indicating I should turn around like some model."

"Agreed."

"Do you have any idea how hard it's going to be to find a white dress this time of year?"

"Not if you know the right places to shop."

Four

The air of the War Memorial Opera House was redolent with perfume. The auditorium echoed with low murmurs, cool laughter and rustling fabric, sounds suited to the exquisite setting. And Lady Luck smiled on Gabriel Marquez.

From his usual box seat he spotted Cristina's brilliant hair as she walked down the aisle ten minutes prior to curtain, Jason's hand resting against the small of her back. Her floor-length emerald green dress was simplicity itself. No glitter for this woman, not even on opening night. Just a classic design that flattered her figure and complemented her coloring.

And he was irritatingly pleased the gown offered little view of her cleavage to the tall, blond man hovering nearby—unlike the gown she would wear for her De La Hoya portrait.

After a great deal of debate the afternoon before, she'd agreed to a champagne-colored silk with skinny straps and a scooped bodice.

Oh, she'd argued against the cut of the gown, believing that a portrait destined to be hung in a family gallery for generations should be tasteful. From behind her, he'd caught and held her gaze in the mirror.

"Who do you look like, Cristina? Your mother?"

"No. Her maternal grandmother."

"And how do you know that?"

"Because her portrait— Oh. I see your point."

"*Your* great-granddaughter will like knowing how she comes by her looks."

"I yield to your expertise, Gabe. However, I don't believe we need to show quite so much 'looks.'"

His body had grazed hers as he moved a little closer. He fingered her dress strap where it touched her shoulder blade. Her flesh tightened under his knuckles. "It will be tasteful enough to hang in the White House."

Gabe recalled the breath she'd held for a long time, then her silent assent. She was pitifully easy to read, and far too open with him for her own good. Plus, she was ripe for an affair, hungry to experience sexual freedom, which was part of the reason she'd embarked on a life independent of her father—even if she hadn't acknowledged it to herself yet.

He understood the risk she was taking—he thrived on risk, after all—but he had to prevent the marriage-merger of Cristina and Jason. Could he do that without sleeping with her? His original plan had included intimacy—the graphically imagined rumpled sheets and morning sun. How else could he entice her away, not only from Jason's persistent pursuit, but from her father's influence?

It was a test of his own character, Gabe decided. Ethics weren't foreign to him, after all. But he had to be very, very careful this time. A seduction—and yet, not. A little heartbreak would be unavoidable, perhaps. Something bearable. Something memorable. Even educational. She wouldn't be so gullible again.

"If you hurt someone for your own gain, the victory is hollow, *hijo.*" He ignored his mother's voice that seemed to speak directly into his conscience, disappointment weighing heavily in the words. However, it wouldn't be his victory alone, but Sebastian's. The reward justified the risk.

Gabe focused on Cristina again as Jason, seated now, pointed to something in the program. She nodded, her shimmering hair bouncing softly.

"This place reeks of money," the woman seated beside Gabe announced.

He took his eyes off Cristina to smile at his companion as he eyed her concession to getting dressed up—a black silk tunic and palazzo pants that she'd probably borrowed. She hated dressing up. In fact, he hadn't seen her wear a dress since her wedding gown years ago. "You look beautiful, Les."

"Save your slick charm for someone who's susceptible, Gabriel."

He smiled leisurely as he stretched an arm across the back of her chair. "I thought you'd be feeling pretty mellow after all the wine you had with dinner."

"Well, I'm not."

He studied her for a minute, then dragged his chair closer and covered her hands, clenched tightly in her lap, with his. "You want to talk about it, Les?"

"No." She blew out a breath. "No, thanks," she said, more gently. "I know you'll listen, Gabe. I just need to work some things out by myself."

"Ben?"

She looked away. "Who else?"

The lights faded. Anticipation built into an anxious silence. Then music washed over them, transporting the audience to another world.

"It's not his fault, you know," Leslie whispered, leaning closer. "It's no one's fault."

Gabe didn't agree, but this wasn't the time or place. "Let the music take you away for a while," he said. He should be heeding his own advice, he supposed, but he watched Cristina instead—and wondered if she was holding hands with Jason Grimes.

Cristina hated her—the woman she spotted with Gabe during intermission. She was tall and model slender. Her short auburn hair framed a face so perfect she didn't seem to need makeup. And she had enough nerve to wear pants to opening night.

Hate wasn't a strong enough word, not when envy and resignation got tossed into the mix, as well. And they looked so…comfortable together, her arm looped through his, her head pressing his shoulder as they laughed together.

Cristina sipped the wine Jason had brought her, before he excused himself, heading in the direction of the men's room. And she waited for Gabe to notice her across the crowded lobby.

Why hadn't he told her he was coming tonight when she'd said she was? Perhaps he was hoping they wouldn't run into each other. Their relationship couldn't be public knowledge because Alejandro De La Hoya was a secret. A dark, magnificent secret.

She shivered and looked away, recalling their shopping expedition yesterday—his interest in each new dress she tried on, his sudden intensity when she'd finally slipped into the champagne silk. His silent and complete approval, communicated by the way his posture turned military, his eyes narrowed and lips compressed. He'd moved behind her, looking in the mirror as she turned side to side.

"Not exactly the stuff of grand portraits," she'd said.

"It's perfect."

His gaze had drifted down her, made a slow return trip, then locked with hers. "Perfect."

Again she'd hoped he would kiss her. Again he ignored her unspoken wish. There was just that feathery touch where her strap grazed her skin. At first she'd thought she imagined it, then heat spread from that one spot. Tentacles of fire flashed down her veins.

"Ready to go back in, Cris?"

Reality yanked her out of the memory. Jason blocked her view of Gabe, who either had not seen her—or didn't want to be seen with her. What did he think, that she would fawn over him in front of his date? He was probably used to that, but—

"I'm ready, Jason," she said, but the enjoyment of the evening evaporated like the fading sizzle of a summer rain hitting a scorched sidewalk.

Gabe watched Cristina until the lights faded again. She'd spent the minute or so before intermission ended looking around the auditorium, something she hadn't done before the first act. He knew the moment she'd spotted him. He pretended not to notice.

Leslie leaned in his direction. "So, who's the gorgeous redhead you've been eyeing all night and pretending not to?"

"You're observant."

"Observing's what I do for a living, Gabe. She's your kind of woman, I think. Do you know her?"

"Her name is Cristina Chandler."

Leslie's gasp was audible above the music.

"Chandler? Are you crazy?"

He squeezed her hand, a silent request for her to hush. "I know what I'm doing."

"You can't— We're gonna talk about this," she whispered, low and urgent. "You are not going to do this."

"Do what?"

"Exact your own revenge. Sebastian asked you to stay out of it."

"Sebastian is looking guiltier every minute, Les. Someone has to buy him some time. And I was responsible for his getting involved in the first place."

A patron in the next box shushed them.

"Let's go," Leslie whispered.

"Can't." He couldn't leave now. Cristina knew where he sat, would notice if he left.

They did leave before the curtain call, however, beating the crowd, then they argued all the way to Leslie's house.

"I suppose you're not coming in," she said when he pulled up in front of her house but didn't make an attempt to park.

"Thanks for going with me, Les."

Her sigh resounded with frustration. "Just be careful, Gabe.

Not only for yourself, but for the innocents who are involved.''

"Sebastian is innocent."

"And so is that woman. Two wrongs don't make a right."

"Right and wrong are often a matter of opinion. You see things in black and white. You are a police detective, therefore you are obligated to enforce the letter of the law even when you don't agree with it, right?"

She nodded slowly. "I suppose."

"I'm not bound by the same restrictions. And I'm doing nothing illegal."

"Perhaps not technically. But what about morally?" She opened the car door and slid out, then leaned back in. "You have a conscience. I've seen it once or twice. Think this through. Please. Before more people get hurt."

"I have. Give Erin my love."

Tempted as he was to just drive off, he waited until she made it safely into her house. He expected he would get phone calls tomorrow from Chase and Ben. She was probably already dialing one of them. It didn't matter. No one would change his mind.

When he arrived home he went directly to his office. Several faxes awaited his attention. After a cursory glance, he put them aside. He strolled across the hall to his bedroom to change into jeans and a sweatshirt, consciously ignoring the question gnawing at him second by second. He took the stairs two at a time to his studio. Hooked over the door was a garment bag containing Cristina's dress, which had been delivered that afternoon, the alterations complete.

He imagined her wearing it, her hair teasing her skin. She had beautiful shoulders and arms, incredible breasts. To hide those features would be criminal.

The human body fascinated Gabe, always had. The muscle and bone of men, all sinew and strength that took every artistic skill he possessed to capture perfectly. The lush curves of women that tempted every sense into a new awareness. His mother had found his stash of *Playboy* magazines when he was twelve. He'd had to show her his hundreds of sketches duplicating the photographs to convince her they were educational tools for him. In the end, she hadn't thrown them out but had enrolled him in art classes.

Of course his appreciation of the female body was sexual, too, but it was incidental to his need to observe and capture the human form on paper, then on canvas. Lately he'd spent little time pursuing that pleasure. However, that was about to change.

He unzipped the bag and freed the gown, then fingered the fabric, drawing it to his nose. It didn't carry her fragrance yet, her distinctive perfume that was neither floral nor musk nor fruity, but something individual and enticing.

He released the fistful of fabric he'd unconsciously clenched, tucked the gown back into the bag, then strode across his studio to pick up his sketch pad. He flipped through the pages until he came across the fantasy of the sea captain's wife. That indescribable expression in her eyes. The purity of her ideals. Then the incongruity of her taut nipples pressing against her blouse. Innocence and allure. A deadly combination.

Arousal came, unexpected and fast and uncomfortable. He closed his eyes, willing it away, but all he saw was her—with Jason's hand resting against the low curve of her back as if it belonged there, as if it had been there plenty of times before. Gabe tossed the sketch pad aside.

The question came out of hiding—were they sleeping together? Right at that moment were they locked in some heated embrace? Was she crying out with pleasure? Was he?

He had to know. He couldn't sleep without knowing.

Not bothering with socks, he slipped into a pair of soft loafers, grabbed his wallet and keys, and was out the door.

Fifteen minutes later he parked in front of her building, a house converted into a two-story duplex. Because it was on a corner, an outside stairway led to the upper floor, her apartment. Gabe parked. And waited. And waited.

Her lights were on, but no one passed in front of the windows. Jason's car was parked four ahead of Gabe's. He'd checked the license plate against the information Doc had given him.

Finally the apartment door opened and Jason came out. Cristina didn't hover at the doorway watching him leave. Why? Because he'd left her in bed?

Gabe studied Jason as he walked to his car. No clues there, except that his tie was gone, his shirt unbuttoned to mid-chest. The moment he pulled away, Gabe opened his door. He took the steps two at a time. Not hesitating a heartbeat, he knocked. He could deal with the truth better than his imaginings.

The blinds covering the long, narrow window beside the door fluttered. A chain lock rasped, metal to metal. The dead bolt clicked. The knob turned. Then she was there, framed in the doorway.

She said his name softly, with obvious surprise and unhidden pleasure. She was fastening the belt of her robe. He looked past her, to her bed. Her still-made bed. He spotted Chinese take-out cartons on her coffee table. Two beer glasses.

"I know it's late," he said inanely. Relief that they hadn't slept together tied his tongue. His mind buzzed as a kind of calm euphoria snaked through him.

Clutching the lapels of her robe, she stepped back. "Come in. I was just changing out of my dress. Give me a couple minutes?"

"Sure."

"Are you hungry? We didn't finish everything. I'd be glad to heat it up."

"No, thanks. A beer would be great, if you have it."

"In the refrigerator. Help yourself." She looked quizzically at him again, apparently wanting to ask questions, then she retreated behind a door.

He scooped the cartons and glasses off her table and carried them to the kitchen, storing the leftovers.

People's refrigerators contained a wealth of information. From Cristina's Gabe gleaned that she liked Chardonnay, vegetarian pizza, Caesar salad, and strawberry yogurt. A half-empty bottle of chocolate syrup sat relatively close to the front, not shoved in back as if forgotten or unused. In her freezer was enough frozen chicken to feed a small army, a single porterhouse steak, frozen french fries, several bags of stir-fry vegetables, pecan halves and frozen vanilla yogurt.

He twisted the cap off his beer, then took a swig as he wandered back into her living area. Her bed sat atop a low platform, the bedspread a big, bold print. Otherwise her furnishings included a couch and coffee table, some cardboard boxes jammed with books, and a multipurpose desk that held a computer, printer, scanner and fax—the minimal home office, except for a five-pound weight resting on each side of her keyboard.

Scattered on the walls were framed watercolors. He moved in front of one, noted the stylized "Cristina" in the lower right corner, then stepped back to study it.

He heard her come up behind him but he didn't look her way.

"I've never seen anything like this," he said.

"The only thing you and I have in common is the size of the work," she said with a nervous laugh. "I had a teacher once who said if you can't paint well, paint big. I'm referring to myself, of course. Not you."

He turned to her, noted her casual attire of leggings and a long T-shirt, then focused on her eyes, which revealed her discomfort at his attention on this personal side of her. "Cristina, these are exquisite. You create images, skeletons, if you will, leaving the observer to fill in the blanks...and to want to be part of the vision you've created."

"I enjoy it. Doesn't pay the bills, though."

"What does?"

She pointed to the computer. "Graphic design. I started five years ago designing logos and advertising layout, mostly for my father's contacts, but I did have to prove myself. Anyway, through word of mouth I've built a nice client list, but my bread and butter comes from designing Web pages. I have to turn down work."

"I'd like to see some."

Cristina was flattered by his apparent approval of her painting. So flattered she forgot to be curious about why he had knocked on her door at midnight. She'd spent the time while she changed wondering at his motives. She kept forgetting how little she knew him because she got lured in so easily by his intense gaze and singular attention, which tempted her.

She walked away from him to sit on the couch, noted that he'd removed the food remainders and thanked him for it. "I'd love to show you, but at another time. It's late, Gabe. I'm curious why you're here. And why you wouldn't acknowledge me in public."

"That hurt you," he said, sitting beside her and putting the beer aside.

"Well, yes. I mean, it's not as if we have any claims on each other. The woman you were with—"

"Is just a friend, and you'll undoubtedly meet her sometime. She wasn't the reason I didn't speak to you tonight, Cristina. To be honest, I didn't want to exchange small talk with your date."

She boomeranged his words back at him. "He's just a friend."

"Whom your father wants you to marry."

"That's true."

"He touched you."

She felt her skin rise in bumps. "*Your* friend had her arm tucked around yours. She leaned against you. You're comfortable together."

"We've known each other for a long time. And I don't stay friends with women I've slept with," he countered quietly. "When a relationship is over, it's over."

The implied warning found its mark. *Go in with your eyes open,* he seemed to say. *I don't make commitments.* So. She had some decisions to make—provided she was reading him correctly, that he was interested in a physical relationship with her.

"Why did you come here tonight, Gabe?"

"I wanted to know if you were sleeping with Jason Grimes."

Her breath hitched. "You could've asked me."

"Would you have answered?"

"You were the one who said I would have no secrets by the time we were done with the portrait. Why waste time evading?"

"You'll answer any question I ask?"

"Yes."

"Why would you do that, Cristina?"

"Because you intrigue me, too. Because I've never met anyone like you. And because I know that what I share will be confidential. You won't betray me."

He looked away, hiding his reaction. She watched him swallow. She affected him, too, she realized. His veneer may be one of sophistication, but he was a human being, with feelings, with emotions. She'd just touched one of them.

"Gabe." She rested her fingers against the back of his hand. The emotionally heavy moment disappeared as he lifted her hand to his lips.

"You shouldn't trust so easily," he said, meeting her gaze.

"Why not?"

"Because you'll get hurt."

Kiss me. Let the pain begin. I don't care. The words were a wish, a command, a need. He didn't seem to hear them. Instead, he stood and walked to the door, stopping there.

"Did he kiss you good night?"

"Yes." Another short, hard, closed-mouth kiss that she'd tried to evade but hadn't.

"If I kissed you, Cristina, we'd end up in bed."

His past relationships obviously had taken direct routes. Attraction—bed. Nothing in between. No courtship. No teasing. While she understood the appeal of relieving frustration, or even curiosity, with sex, she didn't want that with him. Sex without meaning. A temporary measure. If she was only going to be in his life for a short time, it had to mean something more than that—to both of them.

"Have you forgotten the pleasure of just kissing?" she asked, emboldened by the intimacy he created with just his words. She moved toward him.

Gabe watched her approach. He didn't enter a relationship lightly anymore. He made up his mind in a hurry, though, and followed through just as fast. Women today demanded as much as men. But apparently not this woman. How wrong could he have been about her? She was nothing like what he'd anticipated. He should get out now, before he hurt her.

Right. Then she'd be susceptible to her father's pleas, and she'd end up marrying Jason, and Sebastian— He let the thought go as she set her hands at his waist and looked up at him, her innocent eyes enticing him.

"Are you sure you know what you're doing?" he asked, giving her a last chance.

"It's just a kiss."

"You have that much faith in me?" He grabbed her hand, flattened it over the top button of his jeans, then dragged it slowly down. Her eyes widened.

"All we've done is talk…"

"Do you still want to kiss?" he asked harshly.

"More than ever."

He didn't kiss her gently. He devoured her mouth, was flattered at her moans, aroused by the touch of her hands as she slid them under his sweatshirt and up his back. Her fingers were fire itself, hot and sizzling. He couldn't escape the heat pooling low and heavy, demanding to be extinguished. Instead, he curved his hands over her rear and pulled her snug against him, holding her as she raised on tiptoe to align her heat with his.

The kiss went on and on, slanting differently, delving deeper, drawing out needs and wants. The bed beckoned. He wanted to be there. Needed to feel her naked and writhing and—

He let her go. Holding up his hands, palms out, he backed away, grabbed the doorknob and escaped into the cool night, feeling more like some randy teenager, not a man who'd always maintained control.

Her face haunted him all the way home. Those innocent eyes that held a female wisdom he thought he'd understood— but knew now that he didn't.

She was a living, breathing red light. Stop. Here and now.

For an hour he punished himself in his gym, until he pushed

his body into aching mindlessness. Under the shower spray, however, reality returned.

He toweled off and fell onto his bed. The dark room asked him questions, demanded answers. Held him accountable.

He pressed his palms to his eyes, then he reached for the phone.

"Gabriel," the deep voice on the other end said instead of hello. Who else would be calling, anyway? Sebastian was hidden away for a reason. To save his life. Just hearing his voice recommitted Gabe to his cause.

Five

She brought him brownies. A gift. Gabe couldn't remember the last time someone had given him a gift without it being his birthday or Christmas. He was usually the gift giver. Being on the receiving end made him uncomfortable.

A smile on her face, she set the gaily wrapped plate in his hands, hugged him good morning, then stepped back. He had resolved to stay detached. Instead, his mouth watered—for the brownies, and for a kiss longer than last night's. Deeper. More intimate.

He didn't satisfy either craving.

"When did you find time to bake?" he asked as she watched him, her gaze curious.

"I had a little trouble sleeping."

"Cooking is therapy for you?" He set the plate aside, not giving into the temptation yet.

"Not usually." She laid her hand on his arm. "Are you sorry about last night?"

"I lost sleep, as well," he admitted.

"Really?"

"Ah. That pleases you."

"I appreciate your honesty."

Gabe's jaw tightened. Honesty. A word he'd given new meaning to—his own. Qualified honesty. Convenient honesty. It had seemed so easy before he knew her.

"I hung your dress on the inside of the screen over there." He glanced at the tote bag she carried. "You brought a strapless bra?"

"I brought several, just in case. One pushes up. One pushes in. One pushes up and in." She grinned. "And one just sort of props me up."

"Props?"

She shrugged.

Props. His imagination drew him a tempting picture. "May I see them?"

They still had the price tags attached so that she could return whichever ones didn't work, he figured. All four were waist-length and hooked up the front. Two were plain and functional—no frills. One was edged in lace and dotted with tiny satin roses. As for the other...

The other was the one that...propped. It would cover her nipples with fabric, but that's all. The sheer fabric was the exact pale shade of her skin.

"Try this first," he said, passing it to her.

"Somehow I knew you'd choose that one."

He held back a smile. "Although I try, I can't always separate the man from the artist. I'm interested in all of you."

"I've noticed that."

He liked this side of her, the flirtatious, self-confident woman. Had it taken only a kiss to unearth her?

"I gather you went shopping before you came here," he said as she disappeared behind the screen.

"I didn't invite you because I figured you'd get bored."

He heard the amused sarcasm and smiled. "Doubtless."

Cristina draped her skirt on the top of the screen, then her blouse, then her bra, the color of a royal robe. Lingerie was her weakness. She had drawers of it, hangers of the stuff that made her feel feminine and desirable. Then she covered it with sensible garments so that no one would know. But now Gabe would. He would see her sheer purple bra—and know.

The thought excited her, and she was already on edge. His kiss last night had taken her out of herself. She'd never known desire could be so fierce, so unrelenting. So important.

She had decided at about four o'clock this morning while the brownies were baking that she would abandon her inhibitions and let this relationship go wherever it was meant to—even if the heartbreak took a long time to heal after. She'd missed out on a lot of life's experiences. But not this time. Not with this man.

She wouldn't pose nude for him—she would never take that chance—but anywhere else he led her, she would follow.

And maybe she'd be the one he would remember.

Leaning over, she settled her breasts in the bra cups, then pulled the beautiful gown from the hanger and let it drift over her. More like a slip than a dress, it was actually marketed as a wedding gown, one Cristina had argued would look perfect only on a tall, model-slim woman. Alejandro De La Hoya had stepped in, shoving aside Gabriel Marquez, and she'd yielded. He probably didn't know there was a difference between his two personas, but she saw it. Perhaps because she was an artist herself, the slight differences were easy to detect. His eyes darkened, his cheekbones became prominent and his lips hardened subtly when De La Hoya took charge. Gabe the businessman was less intense. Even his voice had a more relaxed quality.

"Should I just go barefoot?" she asked as she emerged from behind the screen.

"Your feet won't show." He'd dragged an overstuffed, oversize, old-fashioned armchair across the room. His back to her, he was in the process of draping it with a huge silk scarf printed in an exotic pattern of green and purple, and decorated with long, gold fringe. He straightened and turned. Gabriel transformed to Alejandro.

"We didn't talk about how I should wear my hair," she said, hesitant. He wasn't saying anything.

He moved closer. "Yes."

"Yes, I *should* wear my hair?"

He smiled, relaxing. "Yes, you look perfect. Exactly the innocent seductress look I envisioned."

"Isn't that a contradiction of terms?"

"Not in this case." He took her hands in his. "Are you innocent, Cristina?"

She'd promised to answer all of his questions, but she wasn't prepared for such intimacy so fast. She drew a settling breath. "Am I a virgin? No. Am I celibate? Yes. And I have been for a long time."

She could see him ask why without saying the word. She hoped he wouldn't ask. Not yet.

He drew her hand to his lips for a moment, then he led her to the chair and slid an ottoman closer so that she could stretch out her legs to the side, forcing her to tip slightly. He guided her to lean an elbow on a pillow atop the arm of the chair, then he brushed one strap down her arm.

She felt the heat of his skin on hers as he slid his fingers behind her low bodice and adjusted the fabric until he seemed satisfied with the way it looked.

Her belly grew heavy in response.

"Comfortable?" he asked.

She nodded.

"If you cramp up, let me know."

"Okay."

He crouched in front of her. Combing her hair with his fingers, he drew it over her shoulders.

"Tilt a little more to your right."

She did, which meant he had to adjust her bodice again.

"Are you sure this will look right for the family gallery?" she asked, a little breathless.

His eyes met hers. "You either trust me or you don't. And remember that you can do with this portrait what you will. Your father doesn't know. It'll be your decision. I think you'll be pleased, however."

"I do trust you."

"All right. These are preliminary poses, anyway. What I do today may not be what I decide to do tomorrow. Be patient."

She would have to work at her computer long into the night, but it didn't matter. He was worth losing sleep over. "I'm in no hurry."

A satisfied smile drifted across his mouth.

"You're not unaffected yourself," she pointed out, letting her gaze drift down his body, then back up. "This is not a wistful sea-captain's-wife pose. So, who am I today?"

Gabe stood and backed away. He scooped up the sketch pad and settled himself on a stool, anxious to get started, needing to ignore the rhythmic pulsing low in his body. Needing to ignore what he was learning about her this time. Sheer purple bra. Matching underwear, he noted through the light fabric of the dress. Celibate. A long time. Too easy. Entirely too easy. And so hard on him, on his commitment to luring her from an obligatory, reputation-saving marriage without sleeping with her.

What kind of a fool's mission was he on?

"Who do you feel like today, Cristina?"

She glanced at the scarf he'd placed on the chair. "I don't know. Maybe I'm living in a harem."

Interesting. "Describe your life."

"Oh, I'm lavished with attention. Live with constant jealousy. Am waiting my turn to be called."

He found a blank page as she spun her story. "You would be prized for your hair color alone," he said. "You wouldn't have to wait long."

"Oh. That's good. I don't think I'd be patient in that situation. And when my time came, I'd be the one to make him forget all the others."

"How?" He watched her eyes glaze, then he drew them. Just her eyes on the empty page. "What skills would you bring that no other woman has?"

"Not just erotic skills. All of the women would be taught the same tricks and techniques. He would admire my mind, seek my counsel, confide in me instead of his advisors."

"You would be resented for that." Her eyebrows now. A low arch, ending in a slight tilt upward.

"He would keep me safe. Guarded."

Gabe enjoyed her fantasies, the old-fashioned belief that love solves all problems. But that's all they were—fantasies. No one had a relationship that good. That perfect. Leslie and Ben hadn't been able to keep their love alive—and there were no two people more suited than they.

"You expect a lot of this man," he said.

"He's my mate. And I'm his. We are everything to each other. Everything. For life."

"He would give up his traditions for you? Would risk being murdered by jealous women or angry advisors who have had their power diluted?"

"Some remain loyal. And he has diplomatic skill. So do I. We would make it work."

"What of the other women? His past? Wouldn't you be jealous?"

"Violently. Yes, of course. I'm human. But his past is that. It has no bearing on the present or the future."

A noble theory, although improbable, he thought. "When did you lose your virginity?"

"The first night I was brought to him."

"No, Cristina. You, not your fantasy."

Awareness blanketed her, changing her expression. She withdrew for a minute, then, "On my twentieth birthday."

A bad experience, he decided, watching her face close up.

"We'd been dating awhile. I thought I loved him, and it just sort of happened one night. He never called me again. I was glad. Every time I saw him after that I just wanted to cry."

"Why?"

"Because I'd given that gift to him and he didn't appreciate it. He took, then he gave nothing." She pushed herself upright. "I never told anyone, not even my best friend, Jen. It's embarrassing."

"To be young? To be foolish? Emotions aren't easy to sort out, Cristina. And people do take advantage. Surely you've learned that by now, if only from that experience."

She stared at him for almost a full minute, then she settled herself in the chair again. "It was painful and messy and I never wanted to let another man touch me," she said harshly.

"But you did, eventually."

She simmered with passion. He knew she couldn't keep control of that forever.

She sighed. "Yes."

"What happened?" He wished he could capture every changing expression on her face, open every window into her soul.

She closed her eyes. "It was worse."

"How?"

"My mother had just been diagnosed with leukemia. I didn't know how to deal with it. I'd been dating this man for months, and I turned to him, in need of comfort. I just wanted some oblivion, you know?" She looked directly at Gabe. "He couldn't— You know. He just couldn't. It was humiliating, not to be desired."

Gabe's grip on his pencil threatened to break it in half. "Why had he been dating you?"

"To get close to my father. To get a job recommendation. I gave up on men after that. My mother's illness took most of my time and energy, anyway."

"But you needed someone to take care of you every once in a while."

"I managed. So, when did you lose yours?"

He admired her for that. For getting past the pain and moving on and not wallowing in what was obviously a devastating experience.

"My fifteenth birthday."

"So young? Well, I hope it was a better experience than mine."

"My father bought me a night with a high-class call girl."

Cristina held her breath. The bitterness that coated Gabe's words told her a lot. "I probably would have guessed that to be every teenage boy's fantasy. But it wasn't, was it?"

"Carnally? Yes. Emotionally? It changed me. Changed my whole life. I am who I am today because of that night and what happened afterward."

She waited for him to go on, but he merely angled his sketch pad differently and worked at a faster, less fluid pace.

"I never told anyone," he said abruptly.

"You didn't brag to your friends?"

He shook his head.

"Why me?"

"I didn't want you to think you're the only one who's been embarrassed or humiliated."

"Were you?"

"It scared the hell out of me." He stuck his pencil behind his ear. "The mood seems to have disappeared. Let's take a break. Have you had lunch?"

"No."

"Sit here for a minute. I'll be right back."

He took the sketch pad with him and was gone only a couple of minutes, returning with a gray-and-black silk robe. "Slip out of the dress and into this. We'll eat on the garden patio, then we'll get serious about working."

He grabbed the plate of brownies and disappeared again.

Cristina tugged the gown over her head. She wrapped herself up in what was obviously his robe, enjoying the way his scent clung to the fabric, wafting up to her nose as she tied the sash and rolled up the sleeves. Barefoot, she padded down the stairs and followed the hall to the back of the house. She pushed open the door and stepped onto the patio. He joined her in a few minutes, a bowl in each hand.

She laughed. "Lunch?"

Gabe eyed his creations. A brownie topped with a scoop of vanilla ice cream, hot fudge sauce, whipped cream and a cherry. "You object?"

"Heavens, no. I bless you a thousand times." She reached for one of the dishes and took a seat on a glider. "Thank you."

"Thanks for the brownies. I ate two of them while I fixed these." He sat beside her. "The best I've ever had."

She made all kinds of appreciative noises after she took her first bite, then she licked the bowl of the spoon, getting every last bit of fudge sauce. "You know, you're very different from what I expected after that first meeting at the gallery,'' she said.

"In what way?''

"Less, um, controlled. Less reserved. I thought you were all surface and gloss, aware of your impact on women, but I was wrong. There are a lot of fascinating layers to you.''

"Everyone has layers. We all choose how much of ourselves to reveal, depending on the level of trust. I happened to trust you quickly. And what do you mean, my impact on women?''

"Aw, come on, Gabe. You've perfected the art of seduction.''

"Do you think so?'' He leaned her way. "Has it crossed your mind that you feel seduced because I was attracted to you—and only you?''

She smiled. "Nope. I watched you turn on the charm for a few others, as well.''

Did he? Had he gotten that slick? He didn't want to think about it. "Not on purpose.''

She let out a gleeful laugh. "But that's exactly my point!''

"I'll only admit that I was attracted to *you* that night. If you'd been alone, you couldn't have gotten rid of me.''

"Thank you. I'm duly flattered.''

He smiled.

"God, this is decadent, Gabriel. Lounging around in a silk robe on a glider overlooking one of the most beautiful gardens I've seen. And eating brownie sundaes for lunch.'' She sighed as she savored another bite.

He set the glider moving gently, rhythmically. They ate in silence, comfortable and restful. He tried to remember the last time he'd seen a woman actually enjoy eating. Either they picked at their food, or if they did eat, they made excuses about having missed breakfast or lunch, like it was a crime to finish a meal. And Cristina didn't utter the dreaded *F* word once, either. He swore if he had to listen to one more woman talk about fat grams...

"Thank you. That was heavenly,'' Cristina said when she set her spoon in her empty bowl, the sides and bottom scraped clean like his. After he took the bowl from her, she leaned her head back and closed her eyes.

"Do you have plans for today?" he asked.

Cristina wriggled her shoulders, seeking a comfortable position. "Uh-uh."

He wrapped his hand around hers and pulled her up with him. "Follow me."

They detoured into the kitchen, rinsed the bowls, then headed upstairs, this time going only as far as the first landing. He opened a door and she found herself in a bedroom—his bedroom, judging by the decor, which was dark and rich and distinctly masculine.

"Nap time," he said, leaning across the bed to fold back the deep maroon quilt.

Nap time? Alone or together? she wondered. Dressed or undressed? The questions held her rooted to the spot.

He straightened, took a good look at her, then smiled gently. "I'll take care of some business while you sleep."

"You lost sleep last night, too."

He brushed her cheek with his knuckles. "My office is across the hall. Come over when you wake up."

She stared at the bed for a long time after he left. Finally she unhooked the not-so-comfortable bra and laid it aside before climbing between the sheets, his robe still wrapped around her. She sniffed the pillow. It smelled of soap or shampoo, something clean and not the least bit feminine. She took stock of the room, noted where three paintings apparently had hung—the hooks still dotted the walls. They must be on display at his gallery. She wondered which ones normally decorated the most intimate room in his home.

With a huge yawn, she snuggled into the blankets and closed her eyes. Just for a little while, she told herself.

She awoke to a dark room. Muttering her surprise, she threw her legs over the side of the bed. "I've slept the whole day."

The clock told her otherwise. Only an hour had passed. But it was dark— Oh. The drapes were shut. He'd come in while she slept and closed them.

Unable to decide whether his gesture was sweet or autocratic, she focused instead on the fact he'd watched her sleep. Not a comforting thought, either. She found the master bathroom, washed up, then donned her bra before seeking him out in his office.

"First thing Monday morning, put in a sell order. For all of it, Erin," Gabe said into the telephone. "You've made a thirty-percent return, sweetheart. Anything else is greedy—and risky. I've been watching it, too, and I think it's headed for a downturn. You can buy again when it's low if you're so stuck on keeping it."

He saw Cristina hover in the doorway and waved her in as he continued his phone conversation. "How about dinner on Wednesday?"

"All *right!*" came the excited voice on the other end.

"I'll pick you up at six. Call me if your mom says no."

"She won't."

"Ask her."

"Okay, okay, okay. Bye."

He cradled the receiver. "My goddaughter, Erin," he said. "She's almost eleven. I got her started in the market when she was six and could read well enough to follow her own stocks in the newspaper. Now she charts them, using a spreadsheet program on her computer. She needs to because she's making a killing."

"With some advice from you."

"Shh. She thinks she's making all the right decisions. She's learning how, even if I'm manipulating the final choice."

He watched Cristina meander around his office, his robe caressing her body, his imagination making demands of its own. She stopped in front of a portrait.

"My mother."

"She's beautiful."

"Yes. Did you sleep well?"

"Mmm-hmm."

"Are you ready to go back up to the studio?"

"Almost."

She sent a flirtatious glance his way. Intrigued, he watched as she moseyed toward him, then planted herself on his desk and dangled her legs alongside his chair. The robe separated a little, revealing pearly skin and a tempting bit of cleavage.

"Cristina?"

"Yes, Gabriel?"

"Is there something you want?"

"No. But thank you for asking."

Itching to shove the robe over and down her shoulders, he linked his fingers over his stomach. Memories of the way she looked tucked all cozy between his sheets, her fiery hair spread out on his pillow, still ate at his insides. "You're sitting on my desk for no reason."

"I have a reason, but I don't *want* anything."

He steepled his fingers against his mouth. "A crystal-clear answer if ever I've heard one."

She smiled. "I've embarked on a journey of self-discovery."

"Have you?"

"I made a promise to myself as I was drifting to sleep."

He waited as she teased him with silence.

"I'm going to try to do something every day that I haven't done before."

"Starting with this?"

"Actually it started first thing this morning, only I didn't realize it. Don't you give me that tolerant-male look, Gabriel Marquez. You take risks all the time, so it must seem silly to you."

"On the contrary, I find it fascinating. I'd deduced that you were raised to behave in a certain way, even before you told me."

"What gave me away?"

"Your clothes, for one. You've been schooled to buy classic designs. Offend no one, right? Don't give anyone ammunition to criticize."

She squirmed. "If you'd added something about never wearing horizontal stripes, you'd have my entire litany memorized."

"And now the rebel inside you wants to be let out to play."

"There's a rebel inside me?"

He stared at her until she looked away, toying with the folds of his robe.

"I wish you wouldn't do that," she said.

"Do what?"

"Figure me out."

He rolled his chair sideways so that he was directly in front of her, then he eased closer and set his hands alongside her thighs. "Which brings us to you sitting on my desk, wearing my robe and very little underneath. And looking sexy as hell."

Cristina tried to shrug. Her feet were touching his shins, distracting her. She wanted to let her legs drift apart so that he could come even closer, but she couldn't take the lead. Everything was new to her. She hadn't really flirted before. Not like this. She didn't even know if she should.

So she waited for him to make the moves.

"We have a problem here," he said.

"What?"

"Look over my shoulder."

She did—and noticed what she'd ignored until then. "Um."

"It's not that my neighbors make a habit of staring into my windows, but I can't be sure."

"I'm covered up."

"I want to change that."

Six

Her mind said "Oh!" but her mouth didn't move.

He untied her sash as if she was the only gift he'd ever been given. She sat frozen in place, letting him. Then he stood, blocking her visibility to anyone prurient enough to be interested in looking through his window. She felt the cool fabric brush her stomach and thighs as he pushed it to her sides. The position wouldn't be her most flattering, especially given where the bra stopped and her panties started, which left some flesh visible between—and even sucking her stomach in wouldn't flatten her abdomen.

Afraid to see his reaction, she stared at his throat.

"You *prop* nicely, Cristina."

Surprised, she laughed. She'd expected him to say something serious, something flattering, maybe even a little romantic. She found the courage to look him in the eye just as he slid his hands behind her back and pulled her toward him, easing her legs apart.

"Shall we try just kissing again?" His words were tight, his eyes dark with promise.

She must have nodded because he kissed her then, an all-out assault against her mouth that she willingly accepted and, when she caught up to him, returned in full measure until he groaned. She needed air— No. What did breathing matter when measured against the thrill that rushed through her like rocket ships launched from her heart into every direction, trailing smoke and flame.

His arms slid lower. Tightened. Invited.

She angled her hips to meet his, silk to denim. Still he kissed her, the intimacy more intense, the contact broken only for a millisecond at a time, their openmouthed kisses erotic beyond her experience.

Touch me. Touch me. Touch me. Her mind screamed the words as her pulse pounded, low and deep and achy, gathering hurricane strength. She had to drag her mouth from his, had to breathe, had to slow things down to feel the experience. To remember. She squeezed her eyes shut as she started to shake. She whispered his name again and again, a plea for him to help her stop shaking. A demand to ease the cresting need.

She felt him drift back, then the robe settling over her. With great reluctance, she opened her eyes.

"We've exceeded your limit of new things for one day," he said, his voice tight. "We should try to get some work done."

Disappointed and relieved, she accepted his help to stand. She brushed her lips across his. "You make me feel so good about myself," she said quietly.

"Don't think I'm doing you any favors, Cristina. I enjoyed every second."

She swallowed. "I needed to know that."

"I'm not that selfless."

"Okay."

When they reached the studio, she retreated behind the screen to change, needing a little time to herself. Maybe tomorrow she'd skip using the screen altogether. He'd seen most of her, anyway.

No. That would be entirely too blatant. What happened between them must happen at his instigation, not hers.

She would never make that mistake again.

There was a limit to what she would risk, after all.

"Cris, wait!"

She'd almost gotten away. Controlling the level of her sigh, Cristina tossed her purse into the passenger seat of her car, then waited for Jason to cross the courtyard to where she was parked. Her father had neglected to tell her that he'd invited Jason and his father to Sunday brunch, a tradition Cristina had never yet dared to break. Her presence was expected. Period.

Jason caught up to her. "Do you have to leave so soon?"

"Soon? I was there six hours."

His hands in his pockets, he glanced over his shoulder toward the Chandler home. "I was kind of hoping we could, you know, spend the evening together."

Cristina stole a look in the same direction. Was there movement at one of the windows? Were her father and Richard Grimes watching?

She should march back into the house and—

On second thought, ignorance seemed safer at the moment. Let them play their games a while longer. She could handle Jason better than she could handle her father, whose fragility surprised her more every time she saw him, now that she wasn't with him daily. It broke her heart to see him looking lost and uncertain after all the years of her believing he was the strongest man on earth. For the moment his valet could care physically for him. But at some point she would have to assume the role of parent. She didn't want that, not for herself, but especially not for him, a man of such intense, personal pride.

"I can't stay, Jason," she said kindly. "I have to get back to the city."

"Do you have a date?"

"No. Just a lot of work."

Again he glanced quickly over his shoulder. "I had a good time Friday night."

"Jason—"

"Sometimes I forget how much I like you," he said, interrupting her. "And how pretty you are."

"Don't." She kept her voice gentle. He really was a sweet man. But he was being manipulated into creating a relationship with her where there was no chance of one happening. She felt sorry for him. At the same time, she wanted to tell him to take control of his own life. Do something. Get a job. "I like you, too, Jason. I always have. But I don't feel...*that way* about you."

"You're not letting yourself find out, Cris."

There were too many questions she wanted to ask—and too many answers she didn't want. Instead she kissed him on the cheek so that he could at least save face with his father, then she climbed into her car. "I'll call you."

She didn't look in her rearview mirror. She focused on the smooth curve of the driveway, then the stretch of road that would take her back to San Francisco from Hillsborough, a long enough trip to give her time to relax. Time to think. Time to convince herself once again that she had a right to her own independent life.

Although she'd used the excuse of work to get out of Jason's invitation, she was too wound up now to sit in front of her computer. She wished she could afford to rent studio space somewhere so that she could paint when she got the urge to, but that was beyond her budget. Maybe three years from now when she came into her trust fund, she could swing it. It wouldn't be a huge amount of money but it could provide a few luxuries that she couldn't afford now.

She didn't plan it consciously, but somehow she ended up at the Galeria Secreto. The Secret Gallery. Why had he named it that? Was it a secret that he owned it? She couldn't recall his name on the invitation she'd received to the opening, but his name hadn't meant anything to her then, either.

She parked and headed for the building, anticipation building. Knowing Gabe was De La Hoya, she wanted to study his work again.

Classical guitar music flowed from hidden speakers as Cristina stepped into the gallery. Raymond greeted her, but she wandered by herself, avoiding conversation with the other patrons, analyzing each portrait with a different perspective now. All but one piece was tagged either Sold or Not For Sale. Among those not for sale was the one she'd dubbed *Sacrifice*, the official title now, according to the discreet sign next to the painting.

She returned to it several times, trying to understand why her stomach clenched every time she looked at it. Her connection with the sacrificial bride went beyond empathy—a century ago she could have been in that very predicament herself. Thank God parents couldn't force their children into marriage today. How unbearable to be in a marriage that was a business deal, not a love match.

Still the image haunted her as she moved on to the largest portrait of the show. A man and woman faced each other in bed, their legs touching, their hands clasped together, as if they'd just made love and were telling each other how much it had meant, how beautiful it was. Discreetly arranged bedding provided modesty, as did the woman's long auburn hair.

"Recognize her?"

Pleasure swept through Cristina at the sound of Gabe's voice. "What a nice surprise," she said, turning to him, accepting a social kiss on the cheek, appreciating that his hand lingered against the small of her back longer than socially acceptable.

"Were your plans canceled?" she asked, staying close enough that they almost touched.

"No. I decided to stop in on my way. How was your day with your father?"

"Fine. Well, tedious, actually. Jason and his father were also there. I felt outnumbered."

"Were they putting pressure on you?"

Curious at the tension that hardened his face, she didn't answer immediately. "I'm adept at changing the subject. Contrary to *your* experience with me, I'm not usually manipulated easily."

"I'm glad to hear that." He gestured toward the portrait. "Do you remember her?"

Cristina scrutinized the piece. "Should I? Is she a celebrity?"

"She was my date on Friday night."

"Really?" She looked closer. "She looks so young."

Gabe chuckled. "Careful. Les already feels she's reached her prime."

"That's not what I meant. She's beautiful—then and now. When was this done?"

"Eleven years ago. She and Ben—that's her ex-husband—had been married for just a year. It was my anniversary gift to them."

"Ex-husband? How sad."

"Sadder still because they have a daughter. I told you about her. Erin. The divorce has been final for a couple of years."

"You're angry about that."

"I'm beyond angry." He stared at the painting. "God, they were happy then. They'd been in love since they were fourteen. It should have lasted a hundred years. And now Erin shuttles between them, and Ben dates, and Les—"

Gabe stopped himself from finishing the sentence. Leslie's pain was her own. He had to respect that.

"Anyway, it's a divorce that shouldn't have happened. I took the painting back. And I put it on display, knowing each of them would come separately to the showing and see it. And remember."

She frowned. "That's emotional blackmail."

"Truth, Cristina. Just the truth. We've been friends for eighteen years. Their daughter is my goddaughter. It gives me rights."

"Remind me not to disappoint you." She held up a hand. "I won't say another word on the subject. I have another question, anyway, if you don't mind."

He welcomed the diversion. "Shoot."

"It's about the painting, *Sacrifice*. The style is a departure for you. Frankly, it looks like a photograph. And it doesn't have the sensuality of the others. There's a starkness to it that implies... Oh, I don't know. A lack of personal interest? Everything else has your touch, your involvement."

They crossed the room to look at the work together.

"I worked from theme, not emotion." He tried to see it through her eyes. If Cristina were as thin now as she had been in the photograph he'd worked from, she might see herself. He was glad she hadn't noticed the similarities.

She shook her head. "You captured plenty of emotion, but it's dark. It lacks the trademark De La Hoya color and fire."

"Her future lacks fire, Cristina, even the wedding night that awaits her."

"You said it was your most recent work. Are you changing your style?"

"I experiment all the time. But, no. This was intentional."

They moved to the next painting. *Sebastian.*

"I like this one a lot," she said. "My first impression was that he belonged in another century, perhaps a landowner in eighteenth-century England. You do body detail so well. His hands are incredible. It's obvious he works with them."

Gabe studied the image. "He's a builder who specializes in restoration and renovation."

"He's also a friend."

He turned to her. "How can you tell?"

"When you looked at the painting, your eyes softened."

Her close observation made him take a mental step back. "I met Sebastian the first day of high school, along with Les and Ben and another friend, Chase. None of us knew any of the others before then."

"Were you in a class together?"

He grinned, recalling the moment. "No, but I'll save that story for another time, I think. Of course, you'd get a slightly different answer depending on which one of us you talked to."

They moved along.

"This portrait," Cristina said, stopping him. "I have a question about this one—just to satisfy my friend Jen's curiosity."

"What's that?"

"She thought the woman had just been, um, satisfied. I thought it was moments away."

His low, sexy laughter melted Cristina's attempt to be blasé.

"Well?" she demanded, refusing to be embarrassed. He'd opened the doors with the questions he'd asked yesterday. They seemed to be sharing their sexual experiences with each other. The woman in this painting could be a part of his past. If so, she wanted to know it. Sort of.

He ran his fingertips down Cristina's hair, grazing her cheek, caressing the shell of her ear as he tucked a strand behind it. He massaged her earlobe between his thumb and forefinger. "What a sensualist you are. I knew almost from the beginning."

She looked around. Only one couple remained as closing time approached, and Raymond was speaking with them. Music muffled their conversation. "How did you know that?"

He leaned closer and whispered, "Body language."

"*My* body?"

"Your beautiful, lush, incredibly womanly body... language."

Genuinely shocked, she pulled back a little. "What did I do?"

"You dragged your wineglass along your lips. You touched your tongue to it, not sipping, just feeling the smooth glass." He pressed her hand between her breasts. "And your other hand was here."

"It was not!"

He smiled with excruciating slowness, his eyes glittering. "Yes, *bella,* it was."

Bella? Bella meant beautiful in Italian, probably in Spanish, as well. She tried not to be unduly flattered, in case it was an endearment he used frequently. But her heart whispered its pleasure, anyway.

"Why do you think I wanted so much to paint you? You epitomize the color and fire you call the trademark of De La Hoya."

She looked away, trying to come to terms with his words. That wasn't her. She wasn't a sensualist. Never had been. Certainly no man had thought so...

Until this man.

She couldn't think about it. Not now. Not in front of him.

"You're not going to answer my question, are you, Gabriel?"

He shook his head, his eyes lit with mischief.

She sighed. "I suppose I should respect your integrity."

"Yes, you should. And since you've so deftly changed the subject, let's change it altogether. I'd like to see more of your work."

"Would you? I don't have room for it at my apartment. It's all at home in my studio there."

"Would you mind taking me?"

There was a new intensity in his gaze, that mesmerizing, not-quite-civilized look she'd observed the first night she'd met him. Why? What possible interest could he have in her amateurish paintings?

"Are you prepared to meet my father? He rarely leaves the house anymore, and I won't sneak in."

"I'd like very much to meet your father, Cristina."

She didn't like the look on his face, something she couldn't put a name to, but which bothered her in some way.

"I'm not sure I want you to see my work, if you can call it that," she said, stalling. The last patrons walked to the front door, Raymond by their side. "I'm not anywhere near your level."

"You are a very difficult woman to compliment."

"I like sincere compliments."

He set his hand on her shoulder. "Before you bite my head off, hold on a second." He turned as the bell over the door jingled. "I'll close up, Raymond. Thank you."

"I'll lock the front door and go out the back," Raymond said with a wave.

Gabe drew Cristina toward the desk, out of view from the street. He turned off the lights, although the office light was on and the door open.

"Let's finish this conversation, shall we?" he asked, inviting her to sit in the desk chair. Her expression bordered on hostile. He wasn't going to let her leave angry at him.

"I do like sincere compliments," she reiterated, her foot bouncing.

"No, you don't." He leaned against the desk. "You don't believe compliments."

"No one can or should believe all compliments. Most of them are empty."

"Not mine."

She looked away from him. After a minute she sighed. "I know."

"Then why are you balking at showing me more of your work? I already told you I think they're exquisite."

"Maybe those were my three best pieces. Maybe what's at my studio is horrendously bad."

"Does my opinion matter?"

She looked directly at him. "Yes. But only if it's honest."

"I guarantee you my honesty."

"Maybe that's what I'm afraid of, Gabriel."

He leaned forward and took her hand in his. The now-familiar gesture comforted and excited her at the same time.

"Take a chance," he said gently. "The old Cristina tested new situations like a swimmer tests cold water—one toe at a time. The new Cristina plunges in."

"How do you know that about me?"

"You've been good about showing yourself to me. It doesn't take a psychic to see that you're reinventing yourself. The conflicts are visible sometimes, but you've been choosing the risky route more than the safe one lately. That says a lot."

The thought passed quickly through her mind that he was having too much influence on her. That he was putting words in her mouth and ideas in her head. And yet everything he said tempted her, enticed her to pass beyond the conservative boundaries she'd stayed within all her life.

Take a chance. The words swirled a while before taking root.

"Okay," she said at last. "We'll go. You'll look. You'll tell me the truth."

"And you'll accept the truth graciously, even if it's positive."

She smiled. "Yes."

"Good. Now, have you done something new today?"

"Not yet."

"Every Sunday night for the past seven years or so I've played basketball with a few friends. How would you like to come along? Maybe even play a bit."

Basketball? She swallowed. "Who'll be there?"

"You can't base your decision on that. It's an adventure."

An adventure. A risk. Another decision. "Well, I don't know a…a bunt from a touchdown, but if you're willing— What's so funny?"

"I like you, Cristina Chandler. And I admire what you're doing."

Tears stung her eyes. She didn't know why—and she definitely didn't want him to see. She stood. "Follow me to my apartment so I can change clothes?"

He hadn't let go of her hand. He tugged her close, instantly wrapping his arms around her, inviting her to lay her head against his shoulder. "Relax, *bella*."

"My life has been so confusing lately." She closed her eyes as he stroked her hair. "I don't know what to do about you."

"Sometimes the best course of action is to follow your instincts."

"Gabriel." She leaned back a little. She was almost nose to nose with him. "My instincts can't be trusted at the moment."

"Why? What are they saying?"

" 'Kiss him. Kiss him better than anyone ever has.' "

"You've already done that. But I don't mind if you do it again."

Her knees went weak. He knew the right things to say, the right buttons to push. And he was patient enough to wait her out. Finally she drew a slow, deep breath. She placed her hands alongside his face and pulled him down to her. And in that split second before their lips touched she acknowledged that this time it would be different. Because this time she knew she was a little in love with him.

But she took the chance, and his mouth settled on hers with the softness of a butterfly testing a flower petal for stability before letting it sustain its weight. Then an invisible force wrapped her up in need, and she locked her arms around his neck and pulled herself flat against him and groaned his name. His hands curved over her rear, lifting her to him, letting her feel his strength. She squeezed her eyes shut against hot tears that trickled out. She'd never known this kind of passion, a passion tempted higher by love. A passion insatiable with need. Still, he didn't touch her breasts or anywhere else that ached for his touch. Oh, he was a master at this. *The* master. And it wasn't going to stop her from enjoying him.

"The game?" he said after a minute.

She moved away from him, trying to find her sense of humor buried somewhere in her emotions. "Just don't say I didn't warn you," she quipped, referring to her nonexistent basketball skills.

"Nor I you," he said, not referring to the same thing at all. He touched a finger to a falling tear.

She nodded.

Seven

"**L**ooks like you've been stood up," Cristina commented hopefully as they entered the dark gymnasium of the Wilson Buckley Youth Center of San Francisco. Her voice echoed back.

Gabe flipped on the lights and glanced at his watch. "They'll be here. We can warm up while we wait."

She eased closer. Grabbing his jacket zipper, she tugged it down with the speed of a lazy snail. Her smile was sleepy. Sultry.

"What did you have in mind, Mr. Marquez?"

Leisurely he grasped her sweatshirt just above her breasts and dragged her to him. He bent his head. Their lips almost touched. "Have you ever even *held* a basketball?"

Her eyes blinked open. "Mood killer."

He smiled as she stepped back and yanked her sweatshirt over her head. His hands closed into fists, which seemed to happen a lot lately. The just-kissing business was more pleasurable than he'd imagined, but the seduction without consummation tested his control with every teasing glance she sent his way, every innocent gesture, every sweet flirtation, so different from the cool sophistication he'd expected.

"If I played basketball in school, I don't remember," she said, bending to retie her shoelaces. "There will be other women playing, right?"

Gabe admired the rear view. "Chase's wife, Tessa."

"Good."

"Who was an all-state guard in high school."

Cristina straightened. "Now there's a confidence builder. No other women?"

"No. Until Tessa, it was an all-guys event—Chase, Ben, Sebastian and me."

"How quickly you forget, Gabriel." A woman's voice reverberated within the gym walls. "I used to play, too."

A string of colorful curses whipped through Gabe's mind. What was Les doing here? She had stopped coming to basketball night since before the divorce.

He took a protective step toward Cristina. Leslie greeted Gabe with a kiss on the cheek, then turned to Cristina.

"Hi, I'm Leslie O'Keefe," she said offering her hand.

"Cristina Chandler," Gabe said. "What brings you here, Les?"

She smiled sweetly. "Ben called to say he and Erin were going to be late getting back from their picnic. I offered to pick her up here so he wouldn't keep you all waiting too long."

I'll bet you did, Gabe thought. She'd hoped that he would bring Cristina to the game.

"O'Keefe," Cristina repeated. "Why do I know that name?"

"Ever been in trouble with the law?" Les drawled.

"Me? Heavens, no. Oh! You're a detective, right? Gabe gave me your name as a character reference."

"Did he? So, how come you didn't check his references? I would've loved to have set you straight about him."

Cristina started to laugh, then realized that Leslie was serious. But they were friends....

Confused, Cristina didn't know what to say.

The sound of a bouncing ball cut into the moment. A dark-haired man approached, basketball in hand.

"Sorry I'm late," the man said. "Hey, Les. This is a nice surprise."

"I'm glad *someone* thinks so."

Frowning, he looked at Gabe, then back. "You're always welcome. You know that. I miss having you here."

Les kissed his cheek. "Thanks. That means a lot. Now, have you met Gabe's new friend, Cristina…Chandler? This is Chase Ryan."

Leslie's hesitation between saying her first and last names made Cristina wonder if she had forgotten it for a second—or if there was some private communication going on. Tension layered the air.

"Where's your lovely bride?" Gabe asked.

Chase broke into a grin. "Tessa happens to be throwing up at the moment."

Leslie reacted first. "Is she—"

"Six weeks pregnant."

"Six weeks?" Gabe repeated as Leslie hugged Chase fiercely. "You must have had a helluva wedding night."

"We did."

As Leslie pulled back to let Gabe congratulate Chase, Cristina saw Leslie's face pale. A split second later she lifted her chin a notch and smiled, leaving Cristina to wonder if she'd just imagined the look of distress on Leslie's face.

"I'll be back in a minute," Chase said, passing the ball to Gabe. "Go ahead and warm up."

He jogged out of the gym, leaving everyone smiling, then suddenly Leslie pressed a hand to her mouth, making a sorrowful little sound.

Gabe set a hand on her shoulder, his expression sympathetic.

"I'm sorry," she whispered. She glanced in Cristina's direction, misery in her eyes.

So, it hadn't been her imagination. Cristina took the ball from Gabe. "I'll just go see if I can throw this thing through the hoop, if you don't mind."

Leslie squeezed her hand. "Thank you."

"No problem."

Cristina kept her back to them as much as possible while she practiced, but she couldn't miss seeing their deep discussion. Gabe wiped tears from her cheeks, and Leslie kept looking anxiously toward the door. Finally, he hugged her, and Cristina could see Leslie dig her fingers into his back. Rocking with her, he looked over her head at Cristina. She couldn't read his expression, something between fury and resignation.

A girl burst into the room and ran toward them. "We're here, Mom! Hi, Uncle Gabe!"

Quiet descended then. Cristina followed their gazes to the door, where a man stood silently, his body tense, his eyes hard. This had to be Ben O'Keefe, the ex-husband.

For every step that Ben took, Cristina matched it. She came up beside Gabe just as Ben did. She slid an arm around Gabe's waist, leaned against him and smiled. "I don't think you'll want me on your team. I didn't make one basket." Then she extended her hand to the newcomer.

"Hi. I'm Cristina Chandler."

He couldn't ignore her, and he wouldn't be rude in front of his daughter, Cristina thought.

She was right. Introductions were made all around, then. Erin tugged Gabe and her father onto the court to shoot baskets with her, leaving Cristina and Leslie to either participate or watch. They opted to sit in the bleachers, a big relief to Cristina.

"Thanks for letting me borrow Gabe," Leslie said. "Is my face all blotchy?"

"As a matter of fact I was just sitting here resenting you because you're such a pretty crier."

Cristina could feel her relax. They both turned their attention to the basketball court.

"I don't want Tessa or Chase to think I'm not happy for them, because I am. It just hit me hard because I've wanted another baby for a long time, and the possibility of that happening isn't looking too great."

"I kind of figured that."

"It's hard, you know?"

Cristina touched Leslie's hand in silent sympathy. Erin shrieked as Ben lifted her to slam dunk the ball.

"I hear your daughter's a Wall Street wizard."

Leslie groaned. "Gabe created a monster. She's got a portfolio you wouldn't believe for someone her age, all started from a bank account he opened the day she was born. He never gives her presents. He puts money in the account, and he also gives her his time, which is priceless. She loves all her surrogate uncles, but Gabe's her favorite. She adores him." She lifted a shoulder casually. "Of course, women do, in general. That's how he got his nickname."

"Which is?"

"Romeo."

At first it seemed funny. Then it didn't. How could a woman trust a man called Romeo?

"How well do you know him, Cristina?"

"We're getting acquainted." She looked directly at Leslie. "You seem to be warning me against getting involved. Or am I reading you wrong?"

"I wouldn't interfere, except that you protected him from Ben, and that said a lot to me. Just be careful. Gabe's not known for commitment to one woman for any length of time."

"What *is* he known for?"

Leslie set her heels on the bleacher seat below. "Well…he's fiercely loyal to those he loves. He's got a photographic memory. He tested well into the genius level in high school. School was incredibly simple to him. I had to study and study and study to make Bs. He listened to the lectures and thumbed through a book—As every time. It would have been really revolting except that he never bragged about it. In fact, he never talked about his grades. He didn't want anyone to know how smart he was. And it's why he's so successful now, of course. His information-gathering skills are superb. But his instincts are impeccable. He doesn't see it as a gift. Sometimes he seems baffled by his success, but I always knew he'd do well." She drew a breath. "God, he'd kill me if he knew I was telling you all this about him."

"All what?"

Leslie opened her mouth, then obviously realized what Cristina was saying—Gabe wouldn't know Leslie had revealed so much about him.

"How did you meet? Gabe says it's an interesting story."

Leslie smiled. "It was the first day of high school. Classes were over. I was headed for home. Gabe flirted with me."

"What'd he say?"

"I don't remember exactly. He was following me. I had hair down to my butt and he made some remark about it. You have to understand that I was a tomboy. Never mind that I had long, wavy hair—my only vanity then—I wasn't into the usual teenage girl stuff of makeup and boys. Anyway, he persisted. I don't think anyone had ever turned him away before. I finally had to knock him down."

Cristina gasped, then laughed. "Was he that scrawny?"

"Oh, no. Not at all. But he wouldn't hit a girl, so he just blocked my punches and kept yelling at me to get off him." She grinned. "Looking back at it, it seems so funny, knowing him as I do now. But then I was furious. And embarrassed."

"Didn't a teacher intervene?"

"We were off school property. Anyway, after a minute or so, Ben and Chase came along. Ben was big even then. He lifted me off Gabe like a speck of dust and kept his arms around me until I calmed down. Chase— God, Chase was reading Gabe the riot act about showing respect for women. Then along came Sebastian, the diplomat. He invited all of us for sodas—his treat—and off we went.

"I can't say we became fast friends, but the friendships were rooted that afternoon and grew through time. Ben and I fell in love that day."

Cristina wanted to know why their marriage broke up. Obviously, Leslie still loved Ben. What had happened that was horrendous enough to split them apart?

"Oh, there's Tessa," Leslie said suddenly, then lowered her voice. "She doesn't look so good, does she? Come meet her."

Cristina followed her down the bleachers. "The only one not here is Sebastian, right? Isn't he coming?"

A few beats of silence followed. "Sebastian is out of town for a while," Leslie said coolly.

What nerve had her question just touched? Cristina wondered. For all that these people had been friends for what—eighteen years?—they were each loners in their own way, sharing when they wanted, knowing they could depend on the others, but content to deal with life basically alone.

Cristina fit in perfectly.

"Every muscle in my body has gone on strike." Cristina groaned as she tried to lower herself into the car a couple of hours later. "You do this *willingly* every week? You are masochists."

Trying not to smile, Gabe helped her in.

"I mean, I walk every day. Up and down hills! I lift weights while I stare at my computer screen. I go to the gym three times a week. I'm not a wimp, Gabe."

"Of course you're not." He fastened her seat belt as she sprawled like cooked noodles. He walked around the car and climbed in. "You were a good sport."

"If Tessa had played, then I wouldn't have had to. Two on two. I only would've been in the way."

"It was good of you to fill in." He started the engine and pulled away. He loved Sunday nights. The world slowed down, even the traffic.

"Good of me? I was ordered."

He laughed finally. "This was your adventure for the day. Once Les and Erin left, and with Tessa needing to lie down, you were all alone. We were just keeping you from getting bored."

"Was that what you were doing?" She slapped her forehead. "Silly me. I thought you were initiating me into the good ol' boys club."

"You kept things civilized. I don't know what Ben would have done if you hadn't been there. He has a nasty habit of venting his emotions on the basketball court." He curved his hand over hers. "I didn't need your protection, by the way, but the gesture itself was appreciated. He was furious."

"I thought that at first, too, then I decided he looked jealous."

Gabe admired her perception but didn't want to pursue it. "Amounts to almost the same thing with Ben. He's the one who wanted the divorce, but he gets jealous when another man touches her. And then there's the guilt."

"The workings of the male mind never cease to amaze me," Cristina said in obvious wonder.

Gabe smiled at her bewilderment. It was as if she'd had too much to drink. She was relaxed and funny, not worried about appearances.

She plucked at her drenched T-shirt. "Whew." She took a good long look at Gabe. "How come you aren't dripping wet? I don't remember a drop of sweat beading up on you. You know, you are the neatest person I've ever met. You still look pressed."

He decided she hadn't meant that as a compliment. "You were checking out my sweat?"

"Oh, sure. Glistening chest and all that. You know. Sex stuff."

He held back the laugh that threatened. "Sex stuff?"

"Don't be dense. It's that stupid myth about women being enthralled by a sweating male. Ha! Sweat's just…just *wet*."

He pulled up in front of her house, turned off the ignition and angled her direction. "Obviously you've never worked up a good sweat during sex. It can add a certain…element, all that slickness, one body gliding against the other."

She didn't say anything for a while, then, "But you don't sweat."

"Everyone does, *bella*. I just wasn't working very hard tonight."

Her mouth opened and closed a few times. "You weren't working hard? Oh, that makes me feel a whole lot better. Thank you so much, Mr. Gabriel Alejandro De La Hoya y Marquez…*Romeo*."

Gabe wondered what else Les told Cristina during their brief but intense conversation. "You aren't going to hold an adolescent nickname against me, are you?"

"I guess all that experience you got on your fifteenth birthday gave you some advantages. I also guess I don't mind that you know what you're doing. That would be a lovely change for me."

The serious turn of their conversation settled a weight on his shoulders. "Maybe you should know more about that night and what followed," he said. "Why don't we go inside and I'll tell you—if you want to listen."

He held her hand, keeping the connection, as they climbed the stairs to her apartment, because he wanted to get back in his car instead and drive to safety somewhere. Anywhere. Part of him regretted offering to set her straight. Another part of him knew it was hypocritical to keep drawing out her secrets without balancing the scales with his own.

And a very small part of him wondered if she'd use his past against him when everything came to a head later. He was arming her. It would be up to her whether to pull the trigger.

"Take a shower first if that would make you feel better," he said as she locked the door behind them.

Cristina debated. What he had to say was much more important than her taking a shower. But she also saw hesitation in his eyes and decided he wanted a few minutes alone.

She squeezed his arm. "I won't be long."

"Take your time. I'll just grab something to drink."

"Pour me an iced tea, would you, please?" She gathered leggings and a chenille pullover from her closet and retreated to the bathroom. When she returned to the living room fifteen minutes later, she found him thumbing through her high school yearbook.

"You weren't a joiner," he said, looking up at her. "You're not anywhere except in the class pictures."

"I was shy."

"You've changed."

She accepted the hand he offered, then sat beside him, their thighs touching. "I never felt that I belonged anywhere. I wasn't a very good student, although I tried. Daydreaming was my best subject. It wasn't until my last year in college that I started forcing myself to get involved with groups." She leaned against him, rubbing his shoulder with her cheek as they looked at her picture together. "And it wasn't until I forced myself to lose all that weight that I realized there was only so much I could change—and so much more that I had to accept. How about you? Were you president of the student body? Captain of the basketball team?"

"I was only interested in making money."

"Even then?"

He closed the book and set it aside. "I had a goal. I could only accomplish it by amassing a fortune."

Cristina wondered if he was aware of how hard he was stroking her hand, the pressure just short of painful.

"I wanted to have the means to destroy my father," he said finally, turning to look at her, his face taut, his eyes dark and fierce.

"And do you?" she asked quietly.

"Yes."

Her heart pounded. She hadn't seen this layer of him. It should have scared her away. Instead, she was fascinated—by his strength, by the power that she could almost see flowing from him. "Will you?"

"I promised my mother I wouldn't."

He was staring right at her, but she wasn't sure he saw her.

"You're not going to keep that promise, are you?"

"He's bringing about his own fall."

"Could you stop it?"

"No."

"If you could, would you?"

"No."

The single harsh word made her shiver.

"Would you care to be more specific?"

"You're lucky, Cristina. You don't know how lucky." He moved far enough away to break their contact. "At least your parents tried their best. At least they were together. Mine never were. My father was married—is still married—to someone else. He cheated on his wife, the purest vow a man makes. He cheats in business. Yet, he is a success."

"Outwardly. He has to sleep at night with his conscience."

"He doesn't have one."

Cristina took a hesitant sip of her iced tea, giving herself something to do as he pushed himself up and wandered across the room. He leaned a shoulder against the window jamb and maneuvered some blinds apart. He stared outside for a couple of minutes.

"My father visited us twice a week." Releasing the blinds, he moved on, stopping in front of one of her paintings, tracing the colorful lines with his fingers. "He and my mother would disappear into the bedroom. Later he'd come out, pat me on the head and leave. Starting when I was eight or so, he'd give me a couple dollars and send me out with instructions on what time I could return."

"Oh, Gabe—"

"Don't." He gentled the abrupt tone. "Please, don't. I'm telling you this so that you understand."

"Understand *you?*"

"That's part of it. But also so that you understand that life is seldom the fairy tale we wish for, *bella.* You were protected, and that's good. But not everyone grows up safe and secure."

She didn't care if he didn't want her sympathy because she needed to give it. She walked to where he stood and slid her arms around his waist, leaning against him. After a few seconds, his arms came around her.

"I don't deserve this," he said, his voice gruff.

She held him tighter.

"Cristina—"

"Just finish telling me." She closed her eyes as he ran his fingers through her hair idly. His other hand pressed low on her back. "Your secrets are safe."

She felt him hold his breath, then let it out in a long, slow stream of release.

"I needed my father. I was at that age where so much was happening to me that I didn't understand. I had this need, this desire to paint. No one else I knew felt like I did, saw what I saw, dreamed what I dreamed. Teenage boys think about sex—all the time. I was as interested in it as anyone. Maybe more. But spending the night with a call girl was not the solution to the problems in my life. If anything, it made things worse.''

He paused, his cheek resting against her hair. "Let's sit down."

"No." She leaned back to look at him. "Let's turn out the lights and lie down."

Eight

Gabe framed her face with his hands and kissed her gently. "Yes."

They pulled the quilt back, then lay on top of the blankets, the darkness inviting his secrets out into the open. She rested her head against his shoulder, and slid one leg between his. He only cared that she was close, that she didn't condemn him. Or pity him too much.

"Thinking about sex and following through on the thought are two entirely different things," he said. "Especially at fifteen. This woman was so sophisticated and terrifyingly beautiful. I felt like a puppet. She worked the strings and I reacted. It wasn't pleasure. It was business."

"I don't know what to say, Gabriel. It's just so sad."

"It was far different from what I'd anticipated when my father announced that he was taking me on the town for my birthday. Hell, it was the first time he'd paid attention to me, much less taken me anywhere. And then to be left in her apartment, him with this pleased-with-himself expression on his face." He felt Cristina shiver. "This is disgusting you—"

"No! I'm appalled, not disgusted. Go on."

He skipped the details. He didn't learn anything that night about pleasuring a woman, only the sexual possibilities. If anything, it stunted what natural interest he had, made him shy away from physical relationships in favor of flirtation. He hadn't had the chance to learn slowly, to experiment, to go a little further on each date until it culminated in making love as the next logical step. It had taken years for him to get close physically with a woman. Years. The nickname Romeo had been such a farce. And no one had known it but him.

He tightened his hold on Cristina, knowing she was waiting for him to continue. "After my father picked me up from her apartment later and drove me home, he handed me an envelope just as I was getting out of the car. In it was a bankbook which showed he'd deposited five thousand dollars in it—for my college education, he said. He'd already done the same for my mother, although a higher amount. Then he left. And he never came back."

"You haven't seen him since?"

"No."

"Did you use the money for college?"

"I didn't go to college. By the time I graduated from high school I'd already made enough money to pay him back, with interest, as well as my mother's payoff. Plus I had a substantial net worth for my age. I didn't figure college would teach me much more about business than I'd already learned on my own."

"How did you make so much money?"

"Studied everything I could about where and how to make it. Took enormous risks. Nothing ever seemed to go wrong. I don't know why."

She recalled Leslie's words about how he never took credit for his success. "Maybe it was because you were smarter and worked harder than the average person, too. So, how did your mother fare through all this?"

"My mother mourns her lost love."

"Still? After all these years?"

"To my knowledge she has never dated." The worst of his

secrets were out, and he became aware of Cristina all warm and soft beside him. He buried his memories quickly and well, accustomed to ignoring them.

"You've come a long way, Gabriel."

"When properly motivated, most people can," he commented, but suddenly became much more interested in the fact that she wasn't wearing a bra. He'd slid his hand under her sweater at some point—he wasn't even aware when—to find a closer connection with her. His fingers sought each bump of her spine. "You're a good listener, *bella*."

"I like it when you call me that," she said so quietly he strained to hear her words. "I like lying here in the dark with you, sharing secrets, touching, holding each other. I feel so close to you."

"No one else knows what you do. No one."

She leaned away from him, which arched her back, which pressed her breasts more intimately against him. "Thank you."

"We're even."

"Except that I didn't share only my horrible experiences, but also my fantasies."

"Shall I share a fantasy with you, *bella?*" Even though the lights were out, he could see well enough to note the encouragement in her eyes, not to mention the fact she slid her hand from his chest to his waist. He cupped the back of her knee and pulled her leg higher, until it rested on his fly, a welcome weight against him as his body responded automatically to her nearness, her scent, her innocent arousal.

"I'm waiting," she said, her voice strained.

He'd been so careful not to touch her beyond the kisses. He didn't think he could stop himself this time.

"The first night I saw you, at the gallery, I had visions of waking up with you, the sheets jumbled, your hair mussed, the sun dancing along your skin."

"It's so hard to believe that you find me desir—"

He covered her mouth with his hand, then pushed her flat against the bed. Rising up on an elbow, he threw his leg across both of hers, keeping her still. "I watched you that night. You with your perfectly acceptable dress that couldn't hide the lushness of your body beneath.'' Hearing her draw a quick breath, he realized he was arousing her when he'd promised himself he wouldn't be so blatant.

And he couldn't stop himself.

''I wanted to come up behind you as you stared at one of the paintings, the one that took hold of your desires and turned them upside down. I could see it in the muscles of your face, in the way your body went taut and still. Even in the way you swallowed. I stared at your dress like it was an engraved invitation. I wanted to strip it away and see if what you wore underneath matched my imagination.'' He trailed kisses along her neck. ''What would I have seen, *bella?*''

Cristina felt her skin rise in bumps, felt her nipples tighten, harden. Ache. She wanted him to touch her. Needed him to. ''I don't remember,'' she said, trying not to beg. Whatever happened had to be because he wanted it, not she.

''Try.''

He moved lower abruptly, pressing his face to her abdomen and inhaling, the rich sound of appreciation filtering through her. Burrowing, he shoved her sweater higher, tasting the skin he uncovered with his tongue as he traced a path upward, discovering her stroke by stroke, nibbling as he went.

Cupping her hands to his head, she moaned her approval.

He dragged his tongue along the underside of her breast. ''What color?'' he asked, his breath hot against her flesh.

''Blue, proba—'' She arched as he used his teeth to tug the sweater higher, freeing her breasts, the dampness creating cool rivers as the air washed her flesh.

''Matching top and bottom?''

''Definitely.''

''Sheer?'' His mouth closed over a nipple; his tongue swirled the hard crest.

''Ah... Um... Or lacy. Maybe both.'' Oh, the things she was feeling! The hot, wonderful, out-of-this-world sensations he created. She wished he would pull off her sweater so that he could touch more easily, taste more freely.

"Let's get this off you," he said, grasping the fabric and peeling it over her head.

How did he do that? He read her mind, saw into her fantasies. At this point, she didn't care how. She just closed her eyes and enjoyed his talented mouth and all the wondrous things he could do with it. The gentle bites, the long, slow strokes. The deep, rhythmic suction that connected her breasts to the very heart of her femininity, now steamy and swollen and in need of satisfaction. Unable to lie still, she rocked her hips. When she would have reached to touch him in return, he grabbed both her hands, stretched them above her head and held them there with one hand.

The needy sounds that came unbidden from her throat brought about a less controlled response from him. He sucked the hard crest of her breast into his mouth at the same time that he dipped a hand between her legs, cupping her, his thumb resting against the sweet, hard place that ached. Stars appeared. Night descended in sudden transformation from day. He released her hands and slid down her, settling his mouth where his hand had been, breathing warm, damp air against her in slow breaths, easily permeating the fabric. She lifted her hips high, pressing herself closer, feeling herself about to fall into an abyss, deep and endless and uncontrollable. The pinpoint of pleasure expanded like a bursting rocket, exploding into the night, all fire and flash, then fading into bits of drifting color.

Awareness returned slowly, and with it the knowledge that he'd satisfied her, but not himself. She laid a hand against his cheek. "Gabriel."

He covered her hand, dragging it to his lips. "I have to go," he said, quietly, tightly.

Disappointed, she didn't say anything for a while, then, knowing she probably couldn't change his mind, she reached for her sweater. She wouldn't ask him to stay. Couldn't. She'd learned from her mistakes. Never again.

He wrapped a hand around her wrist. "Don't get dressed. I'll see myself out. You can just slide into bed."

"I have to change into a nightgown. And lock the door."

His silence made her squirm. Finally he grabbed her sweater and tossed it aside. "Then come as you are."

"Naked?"

"You're wearing tights."

"Leggings."

"What's the difference?" he asked.

"Don't you recognize a stall when you hear one?"

The frustration in her voice made Gabe smile. "It's after midnight. It can be your Monday adventure."

"I can see that I've given you way too much ammunition."

"So, trust me with it, *bella.*" He leaned closer. "The lights are out."

"I can see you just fine," she countered. "And I do trust you."

Guilt tried to creep into his conscience. He refused to let it. So far, he hadn't done much she could fault him for. Nothing irreversible. They'd had fun together. Didn't that count for something? He hadn't anticipated how vulnerable she was, but he'd adapted his plans to suit her vulnerability.

He rolled to the side of the bed to put on his shoes. She didn't budge until he stood and held out his hand. They walked side by side to the door.

"That wasn't so bad, was it?" He waited. "Still feel naked, I guess."

"Totally."

"Are you going to kiss me good night?"

"I don't know."

He smiled at the slightly panicked sound of her voice. He leaned to kiss her.

"I'm feeling things for you that I don't think you feel for me," she said abruptly.

He lifted his head.

"This is serious to me, Gabriel. I'm trying to be some kind of nineties woman, but I'm finding it hard. I don't feel casual about being naked in front of you, although it excites me beyond anything I could have imagined. I don't want you to misunderstand my actions."

"Then perhaps you should explain them to me."

"If I could, I would. I know you're going to hurt me. You've warned me, and I try to remember that. And I seem to be doing things for and with you that last week I wouldn't have dreamed possible." She laid her palms alongside his face. "I'm just not like the other women you've been with, I think."

The understatement of the century, he thought as he set his hands at her waist. "Cristina, will you fault me if I help you become the woman you're struggling to become? To help you experience life the way you've been wanting to? To understand what a passionate woman you are? Or will you condemn me? If that's the case, I'll back away right now. I'll walk out of your life and never see you again."

He shocked himself that he offered her the out. He still had a goal to attain. He still needed to keep her from marrying Jason Grimes. Maybe she was stronger than he thought. Maybe she could resist her father's pleas for help. Gabe didn't trust his instincts any longer.

She didn't answer him, but stood on tiptoe to kiss him. "I'll take my chances," she said against his lips.

He dragged her into his arms and held her until she relaxed. "You have the power to hurt me, too, *bella.*" *More than you know.*

"If you meant for that to please me, you failed."

"That's because you're a better human being than I," he said, backing away and opening the door. The porch light spilled a golden glow on her naked torso for a second, reigniting his desire. "I'll call you tomorrow morning."

The door closed behind him. He heard the locks engage.

He wished he could have stayed.

"I don't know what kind of mood my father will be in," Cristina said as Gabe drove down the Peninsula to her father's home three days later. "He's changed so much lately."

Gabe glanced her way, studying her profile for a second before he looked at the road again. "In what way?"

"When my mother died, he became increasingly demanding of me, keeping me tethered close and trying to structure my life. Even though I understood how lonely he was, I didn't appreciate being treated like a child again, which is why I decided to move out. Plus he became moody and volatile, two words I never thought would apply to him.''

''Do you know why?''

''My mother's death devastated him, Gabe. They were best friends, and now she's gone and he feels lost. Plus, I think he's having financial problems. He won't confide in me, but I do know that the first Chandler to arrive in California was the one who made all the money. The second and third generations were public servants, like my father. I think they believed the bank accounts would refill themselves, somehow. Now all the land has been sold and the profits long since spent.''

She sighed. ''I wish I could give him my trust fund, but it's not legally available to me until my thirtieth birthday. I'm supporting myself just fine on what I'm earning, but I don't have extra for him. At least, not enough to make a difference.''

''And then there's the matter of his wanting you to marry Jason Grimes.''

''Yes.''

He waited for her to elaborate. She didn't, and he felt one corner of his mouth lift in response. She could keep her own counsel, after all. Some secrets he wouldn't be able to drag from her. Or perhaps he could, but he didn't really want to hear them.

''I think he misses the thrill of politics, too,'' she said, turning in Gabe's direction. ''What's your opinion? When a man who's been in a position of great power no longer has that kind of influence, how does he react?''

''It would be a bitter pill to swallow.''

''I expected more than clichés from you. Tell me how *you* would react.''

Gabe couldn't imagine letting himself get in that position, but she would be insulted if he told her that. ''I'd question my own worth. Then I'd find a way to recapture that power.''

''How far would you go to reestablish your place?''

''As far as necessary.''

"I know you'd be willing to take risks," she said slowly. "But would you do something illegal?"

He took his eyes off the road long enough to look closely at her. Did she know what her father had done? Or was she asking hypothetical questions?

"Depends on how illegal," he answered, watching for her reaction. "I've never endangered someone's life. I guess that's my criterion. Why? Has your father done something illegal?"

"Not that I'm aware of. But he seems…desperate." She gestured ahead. "Take the next right, then follow the driveway to the house."

The grounds were expansive and well maintained. He observed Cristina as they traversed the lane, so he saw her tense up and withdraw. They'd spent hours together over the past few days working on the portrait, which was going well. And fast. Too fast. The time flew by as she created a new fantasy scenario each day, giving him more insight into the workings of her mind and keeping the sexual tension between them at an uncomfortable pitch.

Intimacy was building between them, a bond that had taken root in their shared secrets and was threatening to break through the surface and grow into something else.

He stopped the car before the house came into sight.

"What's wrong?" she asked.

He laid a hand over hers, clenched so tightly in her lap that her knuckles were white. "This."

She looked at their hands.

"Are you afraid of your father, Cristina?"

"Of course not."

"Then why have you become like marble? Is it me? Would you rather that I not go with you?"

She shook her head. "You're the first man I've brought home to meet him. He's going to jump to his own conclusions about that. When I called to say I was bringing you, I could tell he was more than a little curious."

Gabe cupped her face, turning her toward him. He ran his thumb along her cheekbone. "Should I be the attentive lover to discourage him from thinking you're going to marry Jason?

Or shall I be a business associate only? Tell me what you want.''

She met his gaze. ''A business associate, I suppose. He needs to keep his illusions, and I don't know how to define you, anyway.''

''Then it's simple. I own a gallery. I'm interested in having you show some of your work, but I needed to see more. Are you ready?''

''Do I get a last meal?''

He smiled. ''I'll play my role, *bella*. He won't suspect a thing.''

Gabe understood that appearances were everything, so he wasn't surprised at the good condition of the house and entry hall. It was only as he followed Cristina to the solarium where her father awaited them that Gabe noticed the signs of disrepair. Since visitors probably didn't come in droves as before, there was little need to spend money where it wouldn't be noticed.

The strains of Verdi drifted their way. So, she'd gotten her love of opera from her father. Cristina glanced over her shoulder and smiled, looking more herself. Her light green sweater and matching wool skirt were appropriate dress for the environment, as were the simple gold earrings, locket and watch. A more traditional artist would have painted her wearing this outfit. The color flattered her, as did the style.

But it didn't say anything about her. Not how vibrant her hair looked against her pearly skin. Nor how smooth and toned her arms and shoulders were. Nor how playful she could be— or how sensual. He was capturing on canvas what was special about her, because she'd opened herself up to him.

He watched sunlight engulf her as she entered a doorway, undoubtedly to the solarium. Gabe followed her in.

''Good afternoon, Father.''

She stopped in front of an elderly man in a wheelchair and kissed his cheek.

Wheelchair?

Gabe's gut clenched. He didn't know... He hadn't been

told... Damn it. Why hadn't Doc included that bit of information?

"Father, I'd like you to meet Gabriel Marquez. Gabe, this is Arthur Chandler."

Gabe extended his hand. "A pleasure to meet you, Senator."

Mr. Chandler nodded as they shook hands. His scalp shone beneath a thin layer of white hair. His wrinkled face reflected a lifetime of public caution, while his eyes sharpened with interest. His gaze flickered from Gabe to Cristina, then back again.

"Cristina told me that you own that gallery that represents De La Hoya."

"Yes, sir. In fact, that's where I met your daughter."

"I've been waiting weeks for an answer about her portrait."

"I already explained that to you, Father." Cristina sat in a cushioned wicker chair and invited Gabe to do the same. "De La Hoya is in big demand."

"Artists." He dismissed the whole breed with a gesture. "Wouldn't know a good business proposition if it sat in their laps."

"That's why they have representatives," Gabe said with a smile, avoiding Cristina's gaze, instead watching her father's gnarled hands as they lay perfectly still in his lap.

"When my daughter called to say she was bringing you here, I assumed you had word from De La Hoya. I gather now that's not the case. So, if that business isn't what brought you here, Mr. Marquez, what is?"

Gabe leaned forward, resting his arms on his thighs. Normally he admired people who were direct, but he knew too much about this man to admire him. Although a minuscule amount of pity had breached Gabe's emotions when he'd first seen the man, he'd squelched it in a hurry. "I'm sponsoring a show for new artists a few months from now. I want to include some of Cristina's work."

Gabe's words jogged a reaction out of Arthur Chandler, but the disbelief that settled on his face only increased Gabe's irritation with him. No wonder she didn't think she had talent.

"Maybe," Cristina inserted in a hurry, cautioning Gabe with her eyes. "*Maybe* he's including me in the show. He needs to see what I've got before he decides. I left most everything here, as you know, Father."

"Thought you'd be back to paint now and then, too."

But you haven't. The unspoken words hung in the air like guilt come to life, a living, breathing accusation.

"Building a career takes a lot of time and energy, Father."

Gabe noted the way she straightened her spine the minute her father reminded her that she hadn't been catering to him enough. Gabe had no personal experience with parental demands. His father had never wanted anything from him, not even acknowledgment. His mother, a kind, timid woman, loved Gabe openly but asked little of him. She had her church and her memories. It was enough, she always said.

Cristina got to her feet. "If you'll excuse us, Father. We'll stop back in after we're done."

Nine

Embarrassment shrouded Cristina as she walked a few steps ahead of Gabe, leading the way to her studio. "I'm sorry, Gabriel. He's usually a little friendlier than that," she said quietly over her shoulder. "I don't know what got into him. He's changed so much."

"Don't apologize for him. I understand him more than you think, *bella*. He's used to having control."

"Not anymore."

"And therein lies the problem." He caught up to her. "Shall I take you to meet my mother? We can compare problem parents."

She smiled, relieved at his acceptance of her father's quirks.

"This is a beautiful old place," Gabe said, looking around. "Did your family build it?"

"My great-grandfather, shortly before his death. I'm a fourth-generation Californian. And now there won't be a son to carry on the name."

"Unless you keep it after your marriage."

"I feel a responsibility to the name, I admit. And so much

of the Chandler history is here, including what was brought from Boston when the pioneering Jacob Chandler made the journey around the Horn. But not to take my husband's name? I don't think I could do that.''

She needed to change the subject. She didn't want to think about what would happen when her father died. The house would have to be sold, the furniture auctioned and the memories put in storage forever, too. There was no brother or sister to reminisce with or to share in the loss. ''Would you like to see the family portraits first?'' she asked, sending an overly cheerful smile Gabe's way.

''Whatever you want.''

She stopped in her tracks. Her breath caught. ''Don't look at me like that.''

He moved close, then rubbed her arms. ''Like what, *bella?*''

''As if you pity me.'' Tears threatened. Life as she knew it was coming to an end. What would take its place?

''What you see is admiration, not pity,'' he said so gently, so tenderly, she wanted to melt into his arms.

''Why?''

''Because you shoulder the burdens of generations, Cristina, and you do it so well. Little from my past matters much to me. Only the present and the future do. I envy you the history you can touch and see and hear.''

''Maybe I'd do better just to ignore it all, to leave it and move on.''

He lifted her hands to his lips. ''You wouldn't be happy.''

Cristina felt the warmth of his breath against her fingers, sending shivers through her. She almost pressed her face into his dark hair so that she could absorb his scent into her skin and breathe it for hours to come. She'd gone beyond being a little bit in love with him, although telling him that would be the same as saying goodbye. ''Stop doing that,'' she said, her voice more shaky than she'd like.

''Doing what?''

''Figuring me out. It's almost creepy the way you see inside me.''

''I'm not seeing any deeper than you're letting me.''

She closed her eyes for a moment, speechless against the truth. What compelled her to reveal so much to him? To trust him with some of the most painful memories of her life?

Because he trusted her with his? No. She'd confided in him first. The irony of her situation didn't strike her as the least bit funny. She'd fallen in love for the first time, and it was with a man who didn't believe in commitment, in the long term, in happy ever after. She hadn't believed either, not for herself, anyway—until she'd met him.

He waited her out, as he had from the beginning, letting her sift and sort mentally without trying to influence her. How could she not love a man who encouraged her to be herself, to know herself, to be happy with herself?

He didn't seem to want anything from her except her time.

Which was a mixed blessing in Cristina's eyes. She wished he wanted her body, because she was more than ready to share it. And that was the biggest risk of all.

"Um, my studio's just down the hall," she said into the long silence, then started walking. "You promised you'd be honest."

"Yes."

Yes. She'd admired his gift for simplicity. He lived in a black-and-white world, she could see that. Things were or they weren't. Could be or couldn't possibly be. An affair ended— period. A friendship endured—period. Loyalty, once given, didn't falter. Disloyalty, once earned, would never be forgiven.

He had the courage of his convictions. She couldn't fault him for it, although she wondered what the repercussions would be for her.

"I'll send a service over tomorrow to take them to the gallery," Gabe said, stacking another painting with the four others he'd selected over the past hour. He'd examined every piece in the room, from her earliest efforts at age six to her most recent.

"You don't have to play the game that far." She folded her arms over her stomach.

He noted the defensive posture, one she'd assumed a great

deal since they'd entered the room. "Despite what your father thinks about artists, you know that business comes first with me. You begged my honesty. How much more honest can I get than to tell you I want to show these in public? To advertise a sparkling new talent? You use color and form spectacularly. Your early work is clearly experimental, but what you're doing now—" He stopped. "You still don't believe me."

"Gabriel, what I do is just so basic. Your work is magic. It's beautiful and erotic and mesmerizing. My stuff is just—" she waved a hand "—lines and curves. Light and shadow."

"Your stuff, as you call it, invites the imagination in to play." He dragged her along with him. "Look at this one. Look at the way she's dancing on clouds, her face full of joy. Or this one. *Hope Springs Eternal,* you should call it—that determined flower pushing through a broken sidewalk." He eyed her directly and saw disbelief still hovering in her eyes. "Why would I lie to you?"

He kissed the bewilderment from her face, a kiss that lacked finesse but teemed with emotion. He felt her relief, first in the way she relaxed against him, then her excitement as she wound her arms around him in iron bands. He ran his hands down her sides, kept them curved at her waist, feeling her flesh stretch as she pulled herself closer. She nipped his lower lip. Nose to nose, they stared at each other, then he dove his hands into her hair and took her mouth violently with his.

She moved wildly against him, hot need pouring from her in desperate little sounds. He slipped his hands under her sweater.

"Gabriel," she breathed, going perfectly still.

She waited, her eyes almost closed, as he brushed his hands across her breasts, feeling lace and hard nipples and soft womanly flesh. He bent his head as he pushed the sweater high, and he caught a taut crest with his teeth. She groaned out his name, long and low and full of need as she arched higher. The lace scraped his tongue. Her fingernails dug into his back.

The front clasp of her bra tempted him enough that he set his fingers there, ready to free her.

Then he remembered where he was.

He set her gently away. The gold flecks faded from her eyes, leaving them dark pools of blue. She breathed through softly parted lips that invited him to plunder again and deeper, to learn the secrets of her body as well as her mind. To savor.

"You make me forget," she said as he finally let her go.

"Forget what?"

She seemed to search for the right word, then finally, "Everything. And you make me believe."

"What?"

"In myself."

God. What was he doing? Guilt tiptoed in. He shoved it back. Not now, damn it. Not now.

"You're a beautiful, successful woman. You didn't need me to point out the obvious."

With both hands she smoothed her sweater. "Oh, I believe in some of my abilities. I'm a success in my chosen field. I'm a good daughter, and a good friend to those few I call friend. But I've never believed I was anything out of the ordinary. You're making me believe otherwise, at least regarding my work."

"Your parents never encouraged you, I gather."

She shrugged. "My 'little hobby.' It didn't stop me from painting."

Gabe winced. "Your father will take notice when he receives the invitation to your opening."

"I've been thinking about that." She turned away and straightened stacks of orderly paintings. "Maybe I should use a pseudonym, like you."

"You've got a name to capitalize on, Cristina. Your name alone will draw your father's friends and associates. It's to your advantage not to hide your identity." He watched her continue to find busy work for herself. "You are willing to part with these, aren't you? Quite a few of my regular patrons want first chance at a new artist, and they won't be happy if we don't put a price on it."

"What if no one...?"

He heard the dread in her voice. "They will."

"You're so sure?"

"I've launched a few careers, Cristina. If this is what you'd like to do, I guarantee you'll make more than a decent living from it. That's how sure I am."

"You're the expert, I guess."

"Exactly."

She grinned. "And humble about it, too."

"Humility is overrated." He glanced at his watch. "I'd like to get a couple of hours' work in on your portrait this afternoon. Are you about ready to go?"

"I need some winter clothes from my bedroom. I'll be back in a few minutes."

He curved a hand around the inside of her elbow, keeping her in place. "I'd like to see your room."

Her brows drew together as she considered his request. "I don't think you'll be impressed, but you're welcome to come along. If you're really good, I'll let you carry my clothes to the car."

"And if I'm bad?"

His words surprised a laugh from her. She opened a door along a side wall and stepped through, not answering him. Wise move on her part, he decided, because over the past few days she had been encouraging him to take their relationship further. Not blatantly, of course, but with subtle gestures and tentative flirtation. He knew the signs. The slight arch to the back that thrust her breasts out a little more. The way she ran her fingers lightly along the low neck of the gown she wore for the painting. The shimmering warmth in her eyes that beckoned him close. Teasing smiles. A toss of her head. Unfaltering response to any request he made of her. The slightly more explicit fantasies she created for him.

She was also obviously waiting for him to take the initiative. How long had it been since he'd been with a woman who hadn't been equally aggressive, equally demanding, if not more so? Cristina's innocence wasn't a lure, he reminded himself. Not a temptation at all.

Damn it. Didn't she know how much he would take from her?

Couldn't she see he wasn't a man who nurtured a relationship, but drained it dry?

Just because he liked her, didn't mean he'd be deterred from his goal. Just because he admired her, didn't mean he'd step back from his resolve to see Sebastian's name cleared and his honor restored.

But also because he liked and admired her, he didn't want her to pay for her father's crimes. How could Arthur Chandler be destroyed without Cristina getting hurt?

She'd already disappeared into a large, lighted closet when Gabe came fully into the room. As with her art, she decorated in minimalist fashion, no frills, no knickknacks. And yet her stamp was there, in the muted floral fabrics and strong colors, and—

Air left his lungs in a rush as he focused on a framed painting along one wall. Hypnotically he moved toward it.

"Gabe? Could you come take these?"

He examined it inch by inch, detail by detail. Smooth, flowing curves, without any angles or lines.

Color. Glorious shades of red and gold. A wash of flesh tone. Blue eyes. Pink lips.

"Gabe?"

A Mona Lisa smile. Invincibility.

"Did you disappear on me, Gabriel?"

Cristina dragged an armful of clothes along with her, then dumped them on her bed. "You *are* here. Didn't you hear me call?"

"I have to have this," he said in a voice she hadn't heard before.

"What?" She followed his gaze. "Oh."

He hadn't moved an inch, didn't even appear to be breathing. She came up beside him.

"Any of the others," she said, staring at the piece with him. "Not this one. This one can't ever go on view."

"No." He turned toward her. Passion gleamed in his dark eyes. "Never. For my personal collection, Cristina."

"I don't think—"

"I'll buy it. Your first sale."

What had gotten into him? she wondered. He couldn't know how personal, how private it was to her. "I can't take money from you, Gabriel. You're already working for free."

"I won't ever show it."

She kept her gaze locked with his, needing to see as deeply into him as he did into her. "Tell me why you want it."

"Because it twists my gut and makes my heart pound and stops my breath." The answer came instantly. "What do you call it?"

"*Freedom.*"

"*Freedom.* Yes. Perfect. Your self-portrait."

Her chin came up hard and fast.

"Painted very recently," he added, not waiting for her to confirm his words.

"Right before I decided to move out."

He nodded. "You wouldn't take the trappings of the past with you. You went bare into the world."

"Almost. You can't leave the past behind completely."

He cupped a hand to her face. She closed her eyes as his thumb brushed her cheek. "Some people can. Just not you. But you shed a lot of your history to make the break."

She swallowed the pain of remembering. "I had to. My father wanted too much from me. I love him, Gabe. I do. I just couldn't take my mother's place. It had to be my turn sometime, you know? My own choices. Even my own failures."

He reached for her and drew her close. She nuzzled his neck, finding comfort in the warm, heady scent of him. His arms promised that nothing would hurt her, his shoulder gave her a safe place to rest. Their bodies touched, arousing but not overwhelming. The emotions were different this time, the need deeper than physical desire.

"It took everything, *everything,* I had in me to paint that. To strip bare and look at myself with honesty and accept what I saw, what I was. To know that this was as good as I get. So many people made comments to me when I was thin. 'You look fabulous, Cristina.' 'I always knew there was a pretty face there.' 'Don't you feel good about yourself now, Cristina?" I just wanted to scream." She burrowed closer to Gabe. "Why wasn't I fabulous before? Or pretty? Should I have hated myself?"

He murmured something soothing. The words didn't matter, only the tone.

"Even on my worst days I didn't hate myself. I look at that painting and fill in all the blank spaces." She pushed away from him. "Yes, I see a body that doesn't need implants to be fashionable. And I see an abdomen that probably won't ever be flat. But I also see strength. Character. Kindness. And hope."

He set a hand at her lower back. "I see invincibility. And an invitation to know you. And beauty that only starts on the surface," he told her. "I also see that I can't take this from you, after all."

She thought about it for a while. "It's just a symbol, Gabe. I am her. I don't need the physical reminder." She looked him right in the eye. "When you're done with my De La Hoya portrait, I'll trade you for this one."

He smiled. "Deal."

"Where will you hang it?"

"In my bedroom."

Where other women would see it? She didn't say the words aloud, but she saw him read them in her eyes.

"I sleep alone, *bella*. Always."

"Why?"

"It's my rule."

Gabe turned away from the question in her eyes to gather the clothes she'd laid on her bed. How could he explain? Sleeping seemed more intimate to him. Sleeping meant not being in control. He couldn't stand the thought of someone watching him as he slept. Yet without a second thought, he'd made her take a nap in his bed. And with conscious thought, he'd gone into the room, violating her privacy ostensibly to close the curtains, but truthfully to look at her in an unguarded moment.

Why? She'd been open and honest with him from the beginning. What had he hoped to see? Some flaws inherited from her father?

He folded her clothing over his arm. A change of subject was necessary. "We're losing the sun, Cristina."

She looked toward the window. "I can send someone up to take the clothes to the car—"

"I can manage."

"If you still want to see the family gallery, we can swing past on the way out. There are only about twenty portraits or so. You can decide if I'm going to fit in with the others or stand out like a centerfold."

He smiled. "I can picture it already. 'Now, darling, please don't pay any attention to that portrait of your great-grandmother Cristina. Some artist took advantage of her sweet, trusting nature.'"

Cristina picked up the story as they walked down the hall. "'See that signature, darling? Really! What more could you expect from an *artist* with the name Romeo? Probably some kind of gypsy, one of those wild, earthy types who thinks nothing of seducing innocent young women then leaving them barefoot and pregnant.'"

A mental picture developed, coming more sharply into focus as he concentrated. Cristina as Madonna. Mother and child. But first—pregnant. Round, soft, maternal, ethereal. He hadn't painted a pregnant woman, although he'd been asked.

"Do you want children, *bella?*"

Her expression showed surprise. "Well, of course. Don't you?"

He shook his head slowly.

"Why not?"

No one had ever put him on the spot about the issue before. His friends knew his decision, but they'd never questioned his reasons. Women came and went faster than the seasons. He appreciated them. He couldn't imagine life without them. But sharing a whole life with one? No one had tempted him to even consider it.

"Did you know that Ben and Leslie fell in love when they were fourteen years old?" he asked.

"I assume that interesting segue has something to do with my question," she said. "Yes, Leslie told me as much."

He nodded. "Fourteen. They had the perfect relationship. When they got married, everyone knew it was for life. They were ideally matched. But the fairy tale ended. If Ben and Leslie can't keep their marriage together, their love alive, who can? Ben is the salt of the earth, a strong, dependable man. Leslie still loves him. But they couldn't solve their problems within their marriage. And do you know who pays?"

"Their daughter."

"Exactly. So why in the world would I want to have children?"

"Your other friend, Chase, took the chance. And you're not Ben, Gabe." They reached the gallery. "But it isn't for me to lecture or advise, is it? I do feel sorry for you, though. Maybe you should paint your own self-portrait and discover your own truths."

"I discovered my truths a long, long time ago."

"Did you accept them?"

He hesitated. "Nothing has happened to change my mind."

"If you're not open to change, it can't happen, either." She held up a hand. "Enough. Come and meet my family. Not a rogue in the bunch, I promise."

He let the change of subject settle for a few seconds. "How disappointing," he said at last.

Ten

Gabe watched Cristina climb halfway up the stairs to his studio before he shut his office door. It wouldn't take her long to change, time enough for him to check his messages and place one call.

He pushed the Playback button.

"It's Raymond. Why isn't your car phone turned on? Call me at the gallery immediately. Big problems."

Beep. A new message started.

"You stretched the bounds of our friendship, Gabriel."

Ben. Gabe stopped sifting through his mail and looked at the machine instead, as if Ben would shoot out like some avenging genie.

"I stopped by the gallery. Took someone along who I thought might be impressed by the De La Hoya magic. But what did I see? My friend had no problem recognizing me, by the way, and she was more than a little curious about who the woman was and how we'd ended up *posing* for the elusive Alejandro De La Hoya."

He dragged out the name like an insult.

"How the hell did you latch onto that, anyway? I thought Les had it. I'm damned sure she wouldn't have given you permission to put her on public display for her fellow cops to drool over. I would've pulled the damn thing off the wall if I'd been alone. I took Raymond aside and told him it had better be gone by tomorrow or I was coming back with a can of spray paint." A short pause. "Call me. Today."

The connection ended with a clatter.

Well, at least Gabe got a reaction, which had been his goal in showing the *extremely tasteful* piece. If Les's cop friends saw it, they'd have nothing more to fantasize on than a carefully draped body. Her eyes shimmered with love, but her body wasn't exposed. The tone of the painting was erotic, not the subjects.

He picked up the phone and punched in a number.

"Galeria Secreto. Raymond Osorio speaking."

Gabe sighed. "Raymond, the point of naming the place 'Secret Gallery' was to intrigue. When you answer the phone with the cheerfulness of a village idiot, the element of mystery is plucked out at the roots."

"Gabe! Your friend, Ben O'Keefe—"

"I know. He already called. I want to know if Les has seen it yet."

"She just left. Came in here with steam coming out of her ears! I was just about to call." He lowered his voice. "You know she carries a gun, right?"

"Did she threaten you?"

"Within an inch of my manhood."

Gabe chuckled. "Go ahead and replace it with the one in the workroom."

"Gladly." A shudder came through loud and clear across the phone line before Raymond hung up.

Gabe made one more call.

"I just met Cristina Chandler's father," he said without preamble. "You neglected to tell me he was in a wheelchair."

"I didn't know," Doc replied. "He doesn't leave the house. Do you want me to dig deeper?"

"Yes. I want copies of medical records if you can get them."

"Right."

Gabe glanced at his watch. He couldn't hear Cristina pacing above him, but he bet she was. He said goodbye and cradled the receiver. Deciding to let Ben and Leslie stew a little longer—and remember a little longer—he left his office, taking the stairs two at a time, an apology on his lips.

The words evaporated. Like a newborn she slept curled up in the overstuffed chair, her cheek resting against her hands.

Gabe slipped off his shoes, leaving them by the door. Scooping up a tablet, he padded over to her and sat on the ottoman. He took his time sketching her, using smooth, quiet strokes, capturing the slumberous tone as much as the woman.

After a while he put his sketch pad aside. Itching to stroke her skin, he carefully rubbed the hem of her dress with his fingers instead, not disturbing what appeared to be a dreamless sleep.

Sometime today it had become critical to Gabe that she not get hurt by everything that was on course to happen. Not by her father's loss of respect. Not by Richard Grimes's destruction.

And not by himself.

His concerns hadn't happened overnight. The first time he'd watched her sleep he'd been aware of how fragile she could be. He'd ignored it then.

Now he knew her better—and was learning more about himself.

She stirred and stretched. Her eyes opened with a flutter, then focused on him. Her smile came slow and easy.

"I fell asleep on you," she murmured. "I'm sorry."

"I kept you waiting too long."

"Business?"

"As usual."

She yawned, arched, stretched farther. "We lost the sun."

"It's all right. You must have needed the sleep."

"Mmm. I've been burning the midnight oil the past few

nights." She snuggled into the chair. Her arms cushioned her breasts, pushing them temptingly higher.

He let her know he appreciated the view. Her eyes held the mysteries of womankind.

Distracting himself, he lifted her feet into his lap and massaged them until she groaned. "Have I been taking up too much of your time, *bella?*"

"Yes. Thank you."

He smiled. "Hungry?"

"A little."

"Did you have other plans for tonight?"

"No." She rolled her head side to side. "Ouch. That nap left me with kinks up and down my body."

He cupped her neck with both hands, dragging his fingers along and down her shoulders. Again. Again. Until she sighed.

"Talented hands, Romeo."

"Why don't you slip into a hot bath while I fix us something to eat."

Her eyes opened dramatically wide. "You cook?"

"Be nice, *bella,* or you won't get dessert."

She put her hands over her mouth like a speak-no-evil monkey, although her eyes danced merrily. He wondered how long it had been since a woman had been playful with him. If ever.

He'd never been the kind of man that women teased. His relationships were direct and uncomplicated—and he liked them that way.

"It's a whirlpool tub," he said, enticement in his voice.

"Ah. My kinks and I sincerely thank you."

"I'll go start the water," he said, standing. "You probably want to hang up the dress here, so I'll be back with my robe in a minute."

Cristina waited until he was gone before she allowed herself the luxury of a long, satisfying sigh. The man was almost too good to be true.

Not that she hadn't seen some flaws along the way—none of them physical—but the imperfections added character and depth. *Superficial* was not a word anyone would apply to him, personally or professionally. His honesty was a rarity in her experience. And he listened. Really listened. As if everything she said mattered. He didn't try to control her, but encouraged her to set her own course.

Of course, *too good to be true* usually preceded the discovery of something patently false. So far, however, he'd been willing to share enough of himself that she knew he wasn't perfect, that he adhered to his own code of ethics and morality. His vendetta against his father bothered her mostly because she thought it was healthier to let go of grudges and old hurts, as she had done. He carried too many burdens.

She pushed herself out of the chair just as he returned, his robe folded over one arm.

"The tub takes a little while to fill," he said. "Stop the water a few inches below the top, then flip the switch that's behind your right shoulder. That'll activate the jets."

"Just wake me in the morning."

He started to leave, then turned around to face her, his expression blank. "Do you want me to bring dinner to you? Or do you want to wait until you're done soaking?"

Possibilities crowded her mind.

"The bubbles will cover you, Cristina."

She dragged the robe from his arm. "A new adventure. Oh, before you leave, I have something to show you."

She draped the garment over the screen, then dug out a photograph from her purse and passed it to him. "I thought you might be interested in seeing what I looked like when I was thin."

After a glance that lasted about as long as a blink, he passed it back to her. "Is there any food you don't care for?" he asked.

When she shook her head, speechless, he left. After a minute, she closed her mouth. No comment? No "You're more beautiful now"? No "Too skinny, *bella*"?

Add *unpredictable* to his list of qualities.

She liked that.

Fifteen minutes after she climbed in the tub, a knock sounded on the bathroom door.

"Cristina?"

"She died and went to heaven," she answered, attempting to sound lazy when everything inside her churned faster than the jets. She was naked except for an unreliable quilt of water. This adventure had turned into a challenge to keep her breasts from rising visibly to the surface. She was losing the battle.

He stepped into the room, which he'd so thoughtfully lit with two fat candles, then he shut the door with his foot, trapping the steam.

"Saint Peter issued me a temporary pass, but it took some prodding." He crouched to set an overburdened tray on the ledge that bordered all four sides of the tub.

Her appetite was nonexistent. She lay still, her arms floating on the surface above her breasts, as he finally looked directly at her.

"I'm in a tough spot, Cristina."

"What do you mean?"

"If I let my eyes wander below your face then look away, you might think I didn't like what I saw. If I touch, you might think I'm overstepping my rights."

"Well, that's just the worst kind of dilemma, isn't it, Gabriel?" She smiled at him. "Why don't you just do whatever you feel compelled to do. I'll try not to misinterpret."

Gabe wondered if she was inviting him to look, to get it over with, to end the suspense. His good intentions had fallen away one by one since the first conversation they'd shared. And tonight the tension that had been building since he'd caught his first glimpse of her would end—unless he stopped it right now.

He had options. He could lay a towel over her. He could move the tray of food close enough for her to reach, then leave her alone. He could make a remark that would let her think she was just one among many, something sufficiently repulsive, like, "I've seen my share of breasts." That would turn her off and ruin the moment.

He opted for the truth, beginning the dance of arousal slowly with her, knowing it would build as the evening wore on. She deserved that much. And if she said no at any point, he'd honor that, too. She already knew he didn't make commitments. And he'd promised himself he wouldn't hurt her.

"I want to know what you look like, *bella*."

"I want to know what you look like, too."

Her retort surprised him. He smiled.

"Go ahead, Romeo. Sit there all smug and experienced and in charge while I'm about as vulnerable as I've ever been."

She sat up, keeping her arms crossed over her chest. He couldn't tell to which degree she was angry or embarrassed or aroused. Perhaps it was the combination of all three that fascinated him. Her cheeks were flushed—but that could be from the hot water.

"I don't believe I look smug," he said finally.

"That's because you don't have the advantage of seeing your own expression."

She was more aroused than anything else, he decided, not knowing why he knew that, but positive of it. He dipped a finger in the water then brushed her lips with the warm wetness. "Why don't you just uncross your arms and get it over with?"

"Why don't you join me?"

He saw the instant regret in her eyes before she looked away. He cupped her cheek and turned her to face him.

"Is that what you want, *bella*?"

"No."

He found her contradictions endearing.

Determined to drag out their time together, however—and to give either of them time to change their minds—he plucked a bottle of champagne from the ice bucket on the tray and poured two flutes. He passed her one.

It was almost funny the way she eyed the glass, then him, then the glass again. If she accepted it, she'd have to stop hiding behind her arms. When she didn't reach for the champagne, he set both glasses down, then stripped off his shirt and tossed it aside.

"Oh, yeah. Now we're even," she muttered.

"Am I to blame that we're made differently? Give me credit for trying."

"This is so silly."

"No." Leaning across the ledge, he kissed her. He assumed the resistance he encountered was tension. "I understand how you feel. Take your time."

Cristina closed her eyes. This was what she wanted, so why was she hesitating? Because no words of love came with the kiss? No big surprise, there, after all. He was used to a much more worldly woman, his equal, undoubtedly.

So get with the times, Cristina. The words bellowing in her head expected action. She reached for a champagne flute, swigged half the glass, then challenged him with her eyes.

"I have a feeling that whatever I say will be wrong," he said quietly.

And with more good humor than she deserved, she thought. He also held his gaze steady on hers.

"I don't need compliments."

"Yes, you do. But I don't think you'll believe me. So why don't we just eat the food and sip champagne and see what happens. Is that all right with you, *bella?*"

He waited until she nodded, then he spread something interesting on a cracker and passed it to her. She accepted it automatically, but found herself too distracted by his chest to eat. He obviously worked out. His arms and shoulders looked strong enough to lift her. She swallowed. When she looked at his face, she caught him shifting his gaze upward, too.

Unfamiliarly aroused by his interest, she straightened her spine. The move tilted her breasts a little higher. She felt her nipples harden as he looked, openly this time.

She licked her dry lips. "You know, beer and pretzels would've been fine."

He rubbed a knuckle down her cleavage, brushed a thumb around one nipple, then the other, his touch gentle and exciting. "This is a special occasion. You're inaugurating my tub."

It took a minute for his words to reach the side of her brain controlling logic. She tried to focus on the conversation. *No other woman has been here before me?* She was supposed to believe that? She studied his expression. "You've lived here for years, you said."

He removed his hand abruptly, then fixed himself a cracker. "Right."

"And you've never used the whirlpool?"

"I shower."

"Then why did you even bother having it put in?"

"Sebastian did the remodeling. He insisted."

Giving herself something to do, she bit into the snack that was disintegrating in her wet fingers, and tried to identify the layered mixture. Sun-dried tomatoes and pesto, definitely. Some kind of creamy cheese. She made appreciative little sounds, then sipped more champagne. "Leslie said something about Sebastian being out of town."

"For a while."

She cocked her head, curious at the instant coolness in his voice—the same way as Leslie's voice had turned icy at the mention of Sebastian.

He stood. "I can see that you're still uncomfortable with this. I'll take the food down to the dining room. You can meet me when you're dressed."

Startled, Cristina watched him pick up the tray and start out the door. "That's the first time you've been wrong about me."

He turned around. "Wrong, in what way?"

"I'd actually relaxed. However, I am starting to feel prune-like. I'd like to get out of the water." She lifted her chin. "But we don't need to go as far as the dining room."

"How far would you like to go?"

The double meaning of his question didn't escape her. "We could picnic—" she almost said *feast* "—on your bed."

A few long seconds ticked away.

"Don't move, *bella*." He disappeared, then came back empty-handed and knelt beside the tub. No one had ever looked at her with such tenderness.

"I feel as if I've known you forever," he said, cupping her face. "I know it's because you've shared so much of yourself so freely. I also know you don't open up like that with just anyone."

She wrapped her hands around his wrists. "With no one.

But you've shared, too, Gabriel. And I don't believe you usually do."

"There is much I haven't told you."

"I know."

"And, as you noted, you're different from any other woman I've known."

"Yes." But what happens after tonight? she wondered. He said he never stayed friends with a woman after an affair. And they had a potential business relationship going as well. Did the fact she was different mean the same rules wouldn't apply?

"If you feel obligated in some way," he said, the words trailing off.

Where love is involved, there is no obligation. But she knew there was a genuine danger—to her heart, her soul and her peace of mind.

"At the rate you keep giving me options? Frankly, I'm more concerned that you're the one feeling obligated."

"Then you know nothing about me."

A flash flood of relief washed through her. It was as close to an emotional declaration as she would get, she decided.

She closed her eyes for a few seconds, drew a settling breath, then she stood. "Would you pass me a towel, please?"

Eleven

Gabe wished she weren't so damned innocent. She looked at him with absolute trust in her eyes, a hopefulness he didn't want and certainly didn't deserve. He'd set out to seduce her, revised his plans after he met her, and now found himself succeeding in his first plan, confirming his sense from the beginning that everything seemed preordained.

He'd let the situation get too far out of hand to turn back now, even if he wanted to.

Which he didn't.

He reached for a towel and wrapped it around her, pulling her against him, trapping her arms between their bodies, delaying the contact of her breasts. So much for good intentions. There was no use dwelling on it, however. What was done was done.

"Are you cold?" he asked, feeling her shiver.

She rubbed her face back and forth against his shoulder. "I'm so excited I can't stand it."

"Nothing like putting pressure on me, *bella*."

"I'm sorry," she whispered. "Can we get started? I don't think I can stand up for much longer."

He wanted to tease her, to make her relax, but he could feel her panic settling in. Added to anticipation, she was beyond teasing.

Keeping an arm around her, he walked with her into his bedroom and shoved the bedding out of the way.

"Turn out the lights, please," she said, not loosening her grip on the towel.

He did. Then he went back into the bathroom to bring out one of the candles. He didn't put it on the nightstand but on a tall dresser a distance away, not so much for light as for atmosphere.

Carefully, he toweled her dry. When he tossed the towel aside she jumped.

"Do you want to stop?" he asked.

"Absolutely not." Surety rang in her voice. "I'm not scared, Gabriel. It's just that…that my whole body is aroused. My nerves are tingling, my skin is a mass of goose bumps, even my hair feels sensitive." She traced his lips with her fingers. "My mouth is watering. My breasts are swollen. *Everything* feels swollen and tender. I didn't know it could be this…consuming. So, don't question me anymore. Just show me."

If ever there was a time he needed control and finesse and patience, it was now. He couldn't muster any of it. He hauled her to him and kissed her, diving his fingers through her hair, cupping her head so he could tilt it farther back and then devour her in the way he'd been waiting all his life. Her moans fueled him, drove him to drag his mouth down her throat, forcing her to arch back, her breasts a remembered fantasy of perfection. He kneaded the soft, full flesh, lifting her toward him as he bent lower. She gasped when he swirled his tongue around her nipple, groaned when he settled his lips over the taut peak, called out when he sucked it into his mouth.

He yanked the buttons on his jeans open, shoved his clothes off and kicked them out of the way, then he slid his hands down her rear and pulled her close. Her body seemed to welcome him with the rightness of destiny. Day to night. Separate to whole.

She shook more violently, her fingers digging into his back, her throat vibrating with little pleading sounds.

Humbled by a reaction he'd never even come close to seeing before, he moved her gently back until she sat on the bed. Before he could follow she flattened a palm against his abdomen, then dragged it slowly down until she could wrap her hand around him, stopping his breath when she explored him with her fingertips.

"I can feel your pulse," she said in a voice laced with awe. "Right here. You feel like life itself. So strong, and yet like velvet."

His head fell back. He breathed deeply. She surprised him with her wonder, excited him with her curiosity, then stunned him by leaning her cheek against his chest and cradling him between her breasts in the simplest, most beautiful gesture he could remember.

"Give me life, Gabriel."

Cristina moved to lie on his bed. His scent clung to the sheets, familiar and enticing. In the shadowy room she saw him protect himself—and her—then he stretched out beside her. Starting at her forehead, he stroked her body, discovering her a little bit at a time. She closed her eyes and enjoyed him—the feel of his body pressed along hers, the whisper of his breath against her hair, the gentleness of his fingers. His leg eased between hers, then as he bent to take her nipple in his mouth, he moved his knee higher, almost touching where she ached to feel it most. She arched and rocked in anticipation. Her body began to shake again, uncontrollably, wildly.

Commands she didn't voice spun in her mind as she felt his fingers glide lower. Lower still. Almost there. Don't stop. Ahhh, there...

She held her breath, savoring the sensations, astonished by how explosive a feathery touch could be. Sounds came from her that she couldn't control. He said nothing, but she felt his equal arousal, his complete focus. The air around them changed, growing heavy with desire. His thumb brushed where she throbbed and her body jerked in response. He shushed her, tension wrapping the words, taut and strained. He kissed her, need replacing the previously gentle caresses. He moved over her with an impatience welcomed and matched by her. Then he mated with her in the most exquisite moment of her life, a powerful merging that made her feel cherished and prized and even loved.

She thought she'd known what to expect, but reality surpassed expectation. Words couldn't tell the story. It was just feeling…all warm, lovely feeling…

Everything changed. Intensified. He cupped her rear, lifting her closer, groaning her name against her hair as he increased the tempo, taking her higher and higher, to a place of new beginnings. Life. He was giving her a new life, a new freedom. The gift was hers to do with what she wanted.

And because freedom didn't come without a price, she held on tight when the indescribable moment ended. She knew she couldn't keep him forever, but he made her feel beautiful and desirable.

He would also break her heart.

"Are you all right?"

His voice came soft in her ear. She nodded.

"Are you sure? You're squeezing the breath out of me."

With great reluctance she loosened her hold. She didn't want him to go anywhere, not even for a second, but he needed a minute to clean up. She didn't pull the sheet over her, although she felt cold without him, and when he rejoined her, he eased her into his arms, sharing his warmth.

"Are you struck speechless, *bella?*"

Don't get serious, she cautioned herself. He won't want to hear declarations of love or even gratitude. Better to avoid the subject altogether, she decided, rather than make a mistake that would drive him away too soon.

"I thought your ego was intact, Romeo."

"This isn't about *me.*"

She nuzzled the hollow of his throat. "It was wonderful. You are wonderful. And I sincerely believe you could tell that without asking me, so let's drop the subject, shall we?"

Gabe rubbed his chin against her hair. What the hell had gotten into him, anyway? Since when did he need validation after lovemaking? Maybe because they'd had enough conversations about sex he expected she would want to talk about this experience. And why did it bother him so much that she didn't?

Because this time was different. He prided himself on his unselfishness in bed. He was always willing to bring a woman to climax more than once before seeking his own satisfaction. But with Cristina, he had wanted the first to be *their* first. Together. No planned seduction, no fail-safe technique, just a simple joining of their bodies and a shared climax. Personal. Memorable. Maybe he should've done things differently. Maybe what he'd done was give himself a memory—but not her.

The doorbell rang. He didn't move.

She leaned away from him. "Aren't you going to get that?"

"No."

"Why not?"

"You're kidding, right?"

The front door slammed. "Gabriel!" The angry female voice came from inside the house and could belong to only one person—Leslie, the only woman with both a key and the alarm code.

He swore as he pulled up the blankets from the bottom of the bed. Footsteps pounded on his stairway.

"I have company," he called out.

"Then get dressed and get your butt downstairs," she ordered through the closed door. "We have business to discuss, and I'm not going anywhere until we do."

"All right, Les. Calm down." He rolled out of bed and reached for his jeans. "She saw the painting of her and Ben at the gallery today," he told Cristina as he grabbed a shirt from the closet. "So did Ben. They're a little upset."

"I'd be a little upset, too, if someone who was supposedly my friend took it upon himself to decide what was best for me. You have to let people find their own way in life, Gabriel. Just because you think they belong together—"

"I know they belong together. And the reason they're so upset is because they were reminded of how perfect they are for each other when they saw the proof in front of their eyes." He leaned across the bed and kissed her soundly. "We'll finish our picnic in a few minutes."

"Gabriel," she said softly, detaining him. "Just because they were suited in bed doesn't mean they were suited in life. Maybe all you've succeeded in doing is to make them want each other, when maybe they'd just gotten over that."

Great. She threw a philosophical argument at him just when he had to go downstairs and face an angry woman.

"Rebuilding starts with the basics, Cristina. You can't get any more basic than sex."

"How about love? That's pretty basic."

"*Bella,* love's the most complicated of all—because it's so damned close to hate."

Cristina watched him leave. Now what? She scrubbed her face with her hands. Would they ever see eye to eye? And then there was that rule he told her about this afternoon, the one about sleeping alone. Which meant an unavoidably awkward moment at some point this evening when he announced it was time to take her home.

She couldn't deal with that.

Not even stopping to retrieve his robe from the bathroom, she scurried upstairs and dressed in her own clothes, then waited.

She heard him call her name, followed by the sound of him jogging up the stairs. She stood at the back window, staring into the night, feeling edgy and embarrassingly close to tears.

"What's going on?" he asked, drawing close, his bare feet hardly making a sound.

"Is Leslie okay?"

"You pretty much nailed it. She seemed to think she'd gotten past missing him, until today."

"Did you apologize?"

"No."

She could hear him shut down. It wasn't any of her business, after all. Maybe their long friendship did give him rights.

They all—Ben, Leslie, Chase, and even the elusive Sebastian—seemed to weave in and out of each others' lives, not always in harmony, but with acceptance that the friendship would endure no matter what.

Unconditional love. It was a rare gift they gave each other, including the right to interfere and to argue, because the anchor held.

"I've got a meeting with a new client early in the morning," she said. "I need to go home and get a good night's sleep."

Silence filled the room for several long seconds, then, "It's eight o'clock, Cristina."

She hadn't looked at a clock. It had seemed like midnight.

"What's wrong? Is this about my interfering with Ben and Leslie?"

Her fingers curled into fists. "I feel raw, okay?" she said at last. "A lot has happened today, and I need time alone to think about it."

"Raw? What does that mean?"

She gestured uselessly, needing to pull back before he did. She'd deluded herself into thinking words didn't matter. She wanted words from him, words of love. Of commitment. It was her own fault for spinning a fantasy around him.

"Explain what you mean by *raw*," he said.

"Exposed."

"In what way?"

Her throat burned. "I don't think I can make you understand."

"Try me."

What was she supposed to say? That she'd fallen in love with a man who didn't know the meaning of compromise, a man who made rules, broke rules and ignored rules as it suited him. If it fit his agenda, he did it. If it didn't, heaven help the person who interfered. She even admired that about him, strange as it seemed.

Or maybe she was supposed to tell him that she'd fallen in love with a man who thought of sex as something basic, not as something soul shattering, as it had been for her. He wouldn't want to hear that.

No, she couldn't explain it to him. She couldn't even look at him. How could she hide emotions that strong, when he saw so deeply and so clearly into her? She needed to let him off the hook, though. He'd been honest, which was more than she'd been.

Gabe waited as long as he could stand it. He had the patience necessary for pulling information from someone. Be quiet for a few minutes and most people needed to fill the void. But Cristina clammed up even tighter. Why? What had happened in the past ten minutes to change everything? Just the way she held her body indicated that something was hurting her.

"Are you trying to pick a fight with me? Do you regret what happened and you don't know how to tell me?" He clasped her arms and turned her to face him. "I hate even asking this, because it sounds so juvenile, but wasn't it any good for you?"

"I already told you it was wonderful. You're very skilled."

Skilled? Is that what she thought? For once, he hadn't consciously used any particular skills. He hadn't felt the pressure to perform but just to be with her, enjoy her. "Then what the hell are we arguing about?"

"You're arguing. I'm stonewalling." A tentative smile followed her words. She slid her arms around him and nestled. "Please don't ask me any more questions."

She had created all those romantic fantasies and described them in detail for him, answered his questions, revealed embarrassing truths about herself, yet she couldn't tell him how she felt now? Now, when what had happened was between *them,* not the result of a fictional creation or a bad experience?

He supposed he should count himself as lucky, that she didn't want to rehash the event. Shouldn't he?

"Do you really want to go home," he asked, "or can we finish our picnic first?"

"I'd like to go home."

Disappointment washed over him. He thought he'd had her figured out. He realized now he didn't have a clue about her.

During the silent drive to her house a few minutes later, he glanced her way when they stopped for a red light. Her posture was rigid, her jaw set, her hands locked together in her lap. He tugged one of her hands loose and pulled it to his lips for a brief caress, then set it on his thigh, his hand covering hers.

At the next red light, he looked at her again and saw a tear spill down her cheek. She turned her head, wiping it away, trying to hide the motion.

Helplessness settled over Gabe. She wouldn't confide in him, so all he could do was guess. He guessed she was sorry they'd taken things so far. He guessed she'd expected more from him. But she hadn't given him a chance to give her more.

By the time they reached her apartment, his frustration had turned to irritation. He snatched the key out of her hand, unlocked her door, then followed her in, shutting the door hard behind him, then turning on a light.

"How the hell am I supposed to fix what's wrong if you won't tell me?"

"Nothing's wrong."

He tossed her keys onto the coffee table. "You cry for no reason?"

Cristina walked away from him, unwilling to get into it with him. "Sometimes."

"Cristina."

Hearing the command in his voice, she turned around.

"You are the most rational woman I know. I don't believe you cry without a reason."

She found she could smile. "I guess that's a compliment. Gabriel, if I could explain it to you so you could *fix it,* as men always want to do, I would. I'm just emotional right now. It's as simple as that."

"That's not simple."

She cocked her head. "I thought you understood women, Romeo."

"I really hate that name."

Frustration resounded in his voice. If she thought it would

help ease his mind to tell him that she'd fallen in love with him, she would. But she knew it would only make matters worse. She'd rather he just thought her flighty.

"I guess I still find it hard to believe you find me attractive. Desirable."

He muttered something she was glad she couldn't decipher, then she went rigid as he moved in on her and grasped her arms.

"You keep telling me that and maybe I'll start to believe it."

"But—"

"When did you think I wasn't attracted to you? I wanted to paint you the minute I saw you. That should have told you something. If you didn't believe that, then you must not have believed that kiss on my desk, when I got so hard I thought I was going to lose it right there, without even being inside you. The last time that happened I was a teenager."

Fascinated, she stared at him. His eyes had darkened ominously, his mouth barely moved because he clenched his teeth so tightly.

"Or perhaps the other night when we were lying in your bed. You don't think I was ready then? Or maybe tonight you didn't notice I wanted you even when you were still hidden by the water. I don't know my own mind—is that what you think? Well, I've got news for you. You fit *my* image of perfection. And I'll be glad to prove it again to you right now."

"How?" Confidence wrapped her with a cloak of daring, the second gift he'd given her tonight.

"I'll show you."

"Tell me first." She tugged his shirt free and slid her hands up his chest. Along the way, she brushed his nipples with her fingertips and felt them harden. Excited by it, she shoved up his shirt and let her tongue follow her fingers' path. "Tell me."

"I'd strip you bare and make love to your entire body until you couldn't stand it for another second. And then I'd bury myself in you and make you scream."

Tension radiated from him. His grip on her arms tightened.

Enjoying her newfound power, she dragged her tongue down the tempting line of downy hair that bisected his abdomen. She teased the flesh above his belt, then she pressed her mouth to the hard bulge below, the denim rough against her lips. His fingers grasped her hair then molded her head, keeping her still.

"Feel how much I don't want you, *bella.*"

Gabe hauled her up. Her scent incited him. Her touch drove him wild. He pulled her clothes away with little regard for fabric or fastenings. She did the same to him. He began his tender assault where they stood and didn't let up, not for a second. She gave him everything, yet he couldn't get enough of her. Honeyed need flowed from her, hot and sweet and breath-stealing as they fell onto her bed. They alternated giving and taking, controlling and submitting, demanding and acquiescing. A whisper here, a stroke there. A slick passage, a powerful thrust. Her legs wound higher and tighter. His mouth caught her scream, transferring the sound deep in his body like an implanted electrode setting off a series of charges, intense and endless. He hadn't felt anything like it before. Not even close. He wondered if he ever would again...

She relaxed under him with a trembling sigh, he collapsed above her with a satisfied groan. They lay like jumbled socks, then he levered himself up and dropped onto his back beside her. He found her hand blindly with his and pulled it along his chest.

"Did I sweat enough for you this time, *bella?*"

Her answer was a husky laugh.

"Tell me you're on the Pill."

Twelve

"I'm on the Pill."

Gabe turned his head her way. Her eyes were closed and her lips curved in a contented smile. "Were you parroting me or are you really on the Pill?"

"You're safe, Gabriel."

He'd never had unprotected sex before. He couldn't believe he'd taken the chance. There had been a moment when he'd realized what he was doing, but...she had felt so good. More important, he believed she would have told him if they'd needed birth control.

"*We're* safe," he said, rolling onto his side and propping his head on his hand. He let his other hand wander over her, not with any intent to arouse but to learn the feel of her flesh, the distinctly female curves and planes. "Relax," he said when she shifted a little. He liked how she sprawled on the sheet, not hiding from him.

After she seemed to fall asleep, he moved so that he could lay his head on her abdomen. Leisurely she began to comb his hair, her fingers massaging his scalp. Contentment settled over him. Her heart beat reassuringly beneath his head. The scent of their lovemaking drifted in the air, a reminder and a promise.

She made a little sound, something between a sigh and a murmur, the tone peaceful as her fingertips grazed his forehead and eyelids, then his lips and finally his jaw. She slid one hand down his throat and across his chest, her touch light and slow and arousing, although he didn't think she intended it to be.

He tried to focus on the tranquility of the moment, but as her hand drifted down his stomach inch by steady inch, the lazy contentment evaporated, one gossamer stroke at a time. "What are you doing?"

"Memorizing you," she answered, combing his hair again with her other hand. "Do you mind? You've always been the one to initiate the contact. Maybe you don't like to be touched…?"

At first he thought she was kidding. He realized she was serious when he felt her tense. "I don't mind, *bella*."

She relaxed. "Me, neither. I'm not used to it, though. My family didn't touch much."

"Neither did mine." He smiled. "And this is different, anyway."

"I should hope so."

He heard the returning smile in her voice, then her hand eased a little lower. He held himself still as the very tips of her fingers brushed him, although she created a breeze with how fast she pulled back.

"Oh! You're…um, you're—"

He waited to see what she would do. Guilt whispered a few choice words to his conscience. Her wonder and innocence should have been given to a man she loved. Instead Gabe was reaping the benefits of her awakening. He couldn't muster enough guilt to deny himself the pleasure she brought—nor did he want some other man to appreciate her surprisingly erotic inexperience. It was selfish—he admitted that much to himself. But he'd never expected to enjoy a woman's innocence, much less treasure it.

His mind shut down as she became more daring. She

worked magic on him with her curious touch. He began caressing her in return.

"Don't distract me." She angled away a little. "I'm not done memorizing."

After a minute Cristina slipped out from under him. The freedom to explore was intoxicating, as was his reaction. There was power in this, she realized. Power to arouse, power to incite, power to satisfy. And it all seemed so easy. When he moaned softly, she knew she'd discovered a pleasure point. When he sucked in a sharp breath, the pleasure seemed to somersault.

She experimented, teased, tested, played. His fists twisted the sheet. His body shook. He also reached the limit of his control.

Muttering a harsh curse, he dragged her on top of him, finding her mouth with his, taking possession as he never had before. A claim that couldn't be broken. A need that wouldn't die. She'd only dreamed of a relationship this perfect, this beautiful, this consuming. Everything had changed. Even the way he kissed her felt different—deeper, harder and yet more tender at the same time.

"You're thinking," he said against her mouth.

She almost laughed. How did he *know* that?

"Don't think, *bella*. Let yourself be swept away." He clasped her shoulders, pushing her up until she straddled him, sank onto him, merged with him.

Her mate. Her one and only. Her partner. He felt powerful inside her, strong and bold and sure. No questions haunted her. No doubts or fears came out of hiding. He cherished her breasts with his mouth, used his fingers to tease where their bodies joined until she arched back, her muscles seizing, her mind empty, her heart full. They rode together on a long trail of mutual delight, stronger than the first time, longer than the second.

Then a moment before she would have collapsed against him, he jackknifed up and held her so hard she thought she would break. She buried her face against his shoulder, and felt his breath hot and fast against hers. Still joined, they rocked and hugged and tried to breathe.

"You are incredible," he said finally.

"No, you are."

"You."

"You."

Cristina leaned back and laughed, unabashedly happy. She loved him. A tiny ray of hope filled her with warmth that maybe he loved her a little in return. Attempting to make a comparison was useless. She hadn't seen him with a woman other than Leslie, so she didn't know how he usually behaved. And her own experiences were no measure at all, not for foreplay, not for the act itself, not for afterplay. She knew only that everything felt right.

"You're thinking again, *bella*."

"Good thoughts." She kissed him, leisurely, tenderly, lovingly. It was easier to keep the words from him this time, because this time she showed him her feelings instead. She hid nothing—not her body and certainly not the stars that must be lighting up her eyes. "I'm like a kid in a candy store who's just been given her first allowance to spend as she chooses."

He laughed, a low, intimate sound that sent shivers down her spine.

"The samples were delightful, Romeo."

In a quick move, he flattened her against the bed. "Better than chocolate, Juliet?"

His whimsy made her smile—that and the fact he was nuzzling her neck. "Are we the star-crossed Romeo and Juliet, Gabriel? Destined to be destroyed because of our families? I hardly think so."

He went still, then he moved off her and sat on the side of the bed. Several seconds passed.

"Your father wants to dictate your choice of husband."

She sat up beside him. "He hasn't actually said so. And I would refuse."

"As did Juliet."

"Did she? I don't remember that. I only remember how quickly they fell in love and knew it would last forever."

He stood. "Forever being a few days, as I recall."

She saw him transform from fire to ice as he gathered his clothes. What had just happened? Why had he changed from lover to stranger in an instant? Because she'd brought love into their conversation?

"It's fiction, Gabe."

"Art imitates life, so they say."

Uneasy, she tugged a sheet loose and wrapped it around her as he dressed. "You're leaving."

He stepped into his shoes. "You said you have an early meeting."

And I sleep alone. The unspoken words hurt. So, he made no exceptions. She was the same as every other woman in his life—not worthy of spending the whole night.

How fortunate that she'd insisted on coming home, after all, because getting out of his bed and being driven home after what they'd shared would have been far too embarrassing. And even more humiliating than her other horrible experiences.

Because this time it mattered a whole lot more.

This hurt. Deep down, into every chamber of the heart, hurt. He could've at least eased out of bed. Maybe even waited until she was falling asleep.

She didn't move as he bent to kiss her.

"I'll call you tomorrow," he said, not making any effort to soothe her, not asking what was wrong. Although since he read her mind so well, he must already know. In fact, he must be used to it. She didn't imagine other women were pleased that he left them in their own beds alone.

"Sure."

"I told you how it was with me," he said, crouching.

"You did." She tossed back her hair and looked him straight in the eye. "I'm fine."

"This isn't goodbye, *bella*. It's good night."

She smiled. "Good night."

Cristina didn't watch him leave. She heard him hesitate at the door, but he didn't say anything. Soon the door latched shut. She stood instantly, hurried to lock the door, then headed for the shower. She didn't cry. Refused to cry. Sex was important to him. Easy for him. No emotion expended, no intimacy shared. A basic fact of life.

She just needed to adopt his attitude. Enjoy sex for what it was, not what it represented. Tomorrow when he called she'd be a thoroughly modern woman, asking nothing of him. A lesson learned the hard way, that's all. Tomorrow she'd be as casual as he.

If tomorrow came.

The sun was rising when Gabe put his brushes aside and stepped back from the canvas to analyze his full night's work. Satisfied, he worked the worst twinges out of his body before heading downstairs. He considered using the whirlpool tub. Instead he took a quick shower, then stretched out on his bed.

Sleep eluded him, along with his peace of mind. Guilt gripped his thoughts like a hawk's talons, painful and relentless. First, Sebastian's injury, which Gabe had indirectly caused. And now, Cristina's disillusionment, a more direct consequence of his temporarily forgetting who she was and why he'd begun seeing her. Hours had passed last night in which he hadn't once considered his goal—until he'd made the mistake of calling her Juliet.

At some point during the long night after leaving her apartment, Gabe came to understand Arthur Chandler and what had motivated him to "sell" his daughter to Richard Grimes's son. A man of Chandler's generation and social status was expected to provide, no matter what. Because the family wealth was gone, and he could no longer provide for his daughter, he did the only thing possible—he found someone who could.

Gabe's understanding, however, fell short of sympathy. Chandler had abused his longtime political standing for personal gain. More important, he was abusing his role as parent by making Cristina a pawn, a person without value beyond that which made her a negotiable commodity.

Ignoring the fact he was doing much the same thing, Gabe rolled onto his stomach and closed his eyes. Still sleep wouldn't come. Thoughts crowded his mind. Thoughts of the kind of man he'd become, the kind of woman his mother was.

Everything was linked to one factor—power.

How one used it defined a person's true character. His mother had been used by a powerful man, and Gabe had seen her resulting scars. And now Cristina was caught between her father and Grimes and himself, a triangle of wealth and power that could destroy her if she wasn't strong enough to fight, self-confident enough to resist. Which man could harm her the most?

Giving up any attempt at sleeping, he dragged the phone from the nightstand onto his bed and punched in a number.

"You're up early," the voice on the other end answered. "Or are you up late, Gabriel?"

"Up all night." God, it was good to hear Sebastian's voice, to remember why he was fighting this fight, one he was on the verge of losing because the unforgivable had happened—the outcome mattered this time. It wasn't money, which could be replaced, that he was risking, but Cristina's faith and trust, and maybe even more. He didn't want to think about that.

He had to think about that.

"Lose a few million overnight?" Sebastian asked through a yawn.

"Not that I know of." Now that Gabe had him on the phone, he didn't know what to say. He couldn't tell Sebastian the truth.

"Can't be woman trouble. You haven't lost any sleep over a woman for as long as I've known you."

"Moral dilemmas," Gabe said at last.

"That's a new one for you."

"Yeah."

"Can't buy your way out of it, Gabe?"

"Not this time. So, how's the therapy going?"

"Slowly. I have more feeling in my legs, though. They're going to start me on the parallel bars pretty soon, although it's like asking a rag doll to dance, I think."

Gabe closed his eyes against the bitterness that came across loud and clear. "You're going to walk again."

"Damn right I am. And so help me, Gabriel, if you say you're sorry, I'm gonna get myself a cab and come see if I've still got a wicked right uppercut. I made the decision to take the job. You didn't pressure me. I knew what Grimes was up to. I could've quit."

"You're an honorable man, Sebastian. More honorable than I. You cared about who else could've gotten hurt. I only wanted to catch Grimes in the act."

"And Chandler. Don't forget him."

A short pause, then, "No. I can't forget him."

After ending the call, Gabe slept, only to be awakened a couple of hours later by the phone ringing. He tried to wipe the sound of sleep from his voice as he said hello.

"Mr. Marquez? This is Arthur Chandler."

Gabe sat up slowly. "Good morning, Senator."

"I'd like to meet with you today. Would you mind coming to my home?"

"I can manage that. Around two o'clock?"

"Two is fine. Goodbye."

Gabe cradled the receiver calmly. He had an unlisted number. What other information had Chandler wanted—and gotten?

He slipped into a robe and walked across the hall to his office. A few minutes on the computer confirmed that someone had run a credit check on him, undoubtedly part of a quick investigation job. He had nothing to hide. He'd never been arrested, and he was solvent, although it would take a deeper trace than had been done on him to find more than the tip of his financial iceberg. His low profile had never garnered much in the way of media interest. No newspaper articles beyond those spotlighting the gallery openings he sponsored. Someone could probably come up with a list of charitable donations ranging from the symphony to the Wilson Buckley Youth Center.

He leaned back in his chair, tempted to call Cristina. He'd hurt her last night, the way he'd left her. As long as he was being honest, he admitted to himself that the whole evening shouldn't have happened. He could have avoided a physical relationship. He'd had plenty of time to consider the pros and cons.

But she filled him with the promise of something wonderful—genuine affection, and an amazed kind of wonderment that was flattering and satisfying.

A simple seduction, he'd thought in the beginning. Not so simple, after all.

And, ultimately, just who had seduced whom?

Thirteen

"**W**hat is your relationship with my daughter?"

Cristina had mentioned she'd thought her father abrupt yesterday. Gabe wondered what she would think today. The man didn't pull any punches. His wheelchair might as well be a throne.

"Cristina explained who I was."

"Cristina—" he said her name slowly "—was hiding something."

"She told you the truth, Senator. I own the Galeria Secreto, and I plan to include her work in a show featuring new artists."

The older man leaned forward. His gaze drilled Gabe. "I know my daughter very well, Mr. Marquez. Very well. She looked at you in a way she has looked at no one else. And you, sir, are not going to tell me differently."

"I didn't notice. I would have no way of comparing her reaction." Gabe didn't move. He returned the man's fierce expression with a mild one of his own. "I can tell you this much. She has a tremendous talent."

"Fluff."

"With all due respect, art is my area of expertise. She has a bright future ahead of her."

"Are you using that line on her, Mr. Marquez? Have you enticed her into bed with a promise of making her a star?"

Gabe watched Chandler's hands clench. Was he concerned about Cristina or the fact he was in danger of losing the only foothold he had—the marriage-merger of the two families? "Do you have so little faith in your daughter?"

"She's a good girl. Always has been. That is until a few months ago, when she decided she needed to move out. Were you behind that?"

"I met her less than two weeks ago."

"Have you dated?"

"We've seen each other a few times. For the most part, it's been about business."

"For the most part."

"I have nothing to say about my relationship with your daughter, sir. You'll have to speak with her."

Her father suddenly looked much older. He'd been backed into a corner but didn't have the strength to come out swinging.

"You come from different worlds," Chandler said.

"We have a great deal in common."

"Perhaps it's difficult for someone like you to understand duty, Mr. Marquez. Cristina has a duty—to her family, to her name. Her public image must withstand the microscope of the media and of those in her own social circle. She has an obligation to those who walked the path before her."

Why? Gabe wanted to ask, confused. She wasn't going into politics herself.

Then the words hit home. "Someone like me?" he repeated.

"The bastard son of an immigrant. Oh, yes, I did my homework."

My name is Gabriel Alejandro De La Hoya y Marquez, and I am descended from kings. He cursed his mother for ever planting the idea in his head. He wanted it to be true now. He wanted to flaunt it in Arthur Chandler's face.

But the truth was that he was the bastard son of Richard Grimes.

Gabe stood. "I don't believe we have any business to conduct, after all."

"I could be of great assistance to you, Mr. Marquez."

Gabe turned around, wondering at the man's game.

"I know you've got your hand in a number of businesses around the city. I still have a great deal of influence in all arenas, whether city, county or state. In what way could I assist you? The zoning commission, perhaps?"

"There is nothing you can do for me. Goodbye."

"You will not have my daughter," he roared as Gabe walked away. "She will marry one of her own kind."

My half brother? Not if Gabe could help it. What degradation would Jason, also the son of Richard Grimes, inflict on Cristina? If he was anything like his father, she'd be in for a lifetime of pain—adultery the least of it.

Gabe returned to where Chandler sat, looking old and frail and desperate, for all his attempts at wielding power. Gabe used his advantage. He didn't crouch in front of the man but towered over him, forcing him to look up.

"Cristina is a grown woman, a capable woman. She'll make up her own mind. And there is nothing—nothing—you can offer me that would make me stop seeing her, even if I needed something from you. Only she has that power."

"If you love her, you'll give her up."

The softly spoken words quavered with emotion. He seemed to shrink into himself.

Gabe could fight power. He could fight being dictated to. But fighting a father's love for his daughter, no matter how misguided, was a battle in which there would be no winner.

"Let her make her own choices, Senator."

"Her own mistakes."

"If necessary."

"I can't," the man whispered. "I can't."

"Then be prepared to lose her. She won't let you tell her how to live her life. I think you know that."

"Cristina will do her duty. That much I *do* know. Good day, Mr. Marquez."

Gabe turned abruptly and left.

He drove a few miles from the mansion, then pulled over under a tree. He leaned his forehead against the steering wheel. For all that Chandler disgusted Gabe, admiration balanced the disgust. He was her father. He loved her, wanted to protect her, wanted to secure her future before he died.

He was just going about it all wrong. Gabe didn't respond to threats. Never had. Never would. He reacted. He confronted. He came out the winner. Always.

Leaning his head back against the headrest, he stared at nothing, then he pushed a button, opening the sun roof, needing the fresh air. How was she going to be able to fight? Her father looked on the verge of dying. How could she resist any request he made?

Gabe had to convince her otherwise. Maybe even tell her the truth. Chances were that her father had already called Richard Grimes by now.

The clock ticked—for all of them.

He started the engine and pulled onto the road, barely aware of his surroundings. His car phone chirped. Gabe punched a button on the visor.

"Yes?"

"It's Doc. I got the information you wanted. Cancer of the spine. Inoperable."

Gabe cut the connection. He drove a few more miles as he let his mind fill with every possible curse known to man, and then he made up a few more. When the curses all spilled out, he was left with an emptiness into which an image of Cristina flowed—alone and sad. Lost.

He dialed a number and waited as it rang. Once, twice, three times. On the sixth ring she answered.

"Hello?"

"It's Gabe."

"Oh, hi. How are you?"

He heard the forced cheerfulness.

"May I stop by?" he asked.

He had to ask her to repeat her answer because static covered her words the first time. He gripped the steering wheel hard enough to crack it until she said he was welcome to stop by.

"I'm about an hour away, with traffic."

"Okay. See you."

An hour. He had an hour to decide what the hell he was going to say to her. An hour. A lifetime.

Cristina left her computer turned on so that it looked like she was working and didn't expect him to stay long. What had started as the best night of her life had deteriorated into one of the worst, and the bright light of day had brought the need to analyze her situation.

First of all she needed to face some facts. Her first impression of Gabe had been that he was not quite civilized. He'd confirmed that impression in a big way. He conducted a civilized business, presented a civilized facade. But he was also driven and manipulative, even if he did justify his actions with good intentions, as with Ben and Leslie.

He said he wouldn't stop his father's downfall, even if he could.

What else? That he would resort to almost anything to recapture power if he lost it. And he hadn't apologized to Leslie—therefore, he probably didn't apologize to anyone.

Gabriel Marquez saw the world from between blinders of his own making. And yet it wasn't all grim, either. He was staunchly loyal, pleased that he could help others, and a good listener, a caring listener. A ten-year-old girl loved him the best of all her surrogate uncles.

And he made this twenty-seven-year-old feel like the most beautiful woman in the world.

Cristina was attracted to his dangerous edge. She'd never denied it was part of his allure. She just didn't want to give him up, which seemed inevitable, given his track record. So, in order to keep him interested, she had to change her own attitude. Become blasé, accept him as he was, as he seemed to accept her. She didn't want to act differently around him, but she felt different—so was that dishonest? She didn't know.

Her heart pounded as she heard him climb her stairs. She would greet him casually. Drawing a deep breath, she tossed her hair back and turned the doorknob.

He didn't smile, didn't say a word. He just stared at her for so long that she finally had to breathe again. Then he stepped into the room, shoved the door shut and took her into his arms, holding her until she felt a part of him. She heard him breathe, felt him shudder. Warmth seeped from him, as did a sense of rightness that obliterated her doubts.

"I'm sorry about last night," he said, his voice somber.

"Last night was wonderful."

"I mean about leaving you so abruptly."

"Oh, that. It was fine."

He leaned back without releasing her. "No, it wasn't. I hurt you, and I'm sorry."

Hadn't she just decided he never apologized? Unpredictable man. He looked so…fierce, so serious. Maybe she was turning his life upside down, too. Whatever the reason, she took pity on him.

"I'm fine. Really, Gabe. Kiss me hello and all will be forgiven."

The kiss started urgently then turned tender and sweet and memorable in its simplicity.

"I can't figure you out," she said with a sigh as he finally took a step back.

His smile came slowly and was tinged with something she couldn't identify. Sadness? Pity? She hoped not pity.

"How did your meeting go?" he asked, taking her hand and walking with her to the couch.

As soon as they sat down, he put his arm around her, pulling her close enough to rest her head against his shoulder, their bodies touching. She shut her eyes and snuggled closer, wrapping an arm around his waist. "My meeting was fabulous, thank you. I get to do my favorite kind of job—design a company logo. Well, update one, actually. But I love creating a symbol that represents a company's image and goals and history, all in one.''

"I want to make love to you."

Cristina heard his heart rate soar. "What's stopping you?"

"I don't want you to think that's the only reason I'm here."

Was he kidding? She would be incredibly flattered if that *were* the only reason. Her confidence skyrocketed, even though the sun hadn't quite set yet and the room would be filled with enough light that he could see her clearly.

"Right after you called I took a shower," she said, drawing back to look at him. "I put on a silky little something I hoped you would see and enjoy. I guess we both want the same thing."

Gabe eyed her plain sweatshirt and jeans, wondering what bit of temptation they hid. His anticipation surprised him almost as much as his reaction to her when she'd first opened the door. She'd seemed so fragile that he wanted to hide her away someplace until everything was resolved. All he could do was let his body be her shield, his arms her protection. So much was happening around her, and he was as guilty as the others for keeping her in the dark.

"Shall I show you?" she asked, then didn't wait for an answer. Instead, she walked to the front door first and closed the blinds, then she shut down her computer. She didn't put on a performance, but simply pushed off her jeans and peeled the sweatshirt over her head, unveiling an emerald green lace teddy that revealed more of her voluptuous body than it hid.

Standing, he stripped away his clothes, took her hand and led her to bed, wishing he could change everything—except meeting her.

She didn't lie down beside him but knelt, the narrow straps of her teddy drifting down her arms, the low bodice catching on her nipples, a teasing, tempting sight. She leaned over and kissed him, her open mouth hot and demanding, the lace-covered tips of her breasts brushing his chest.

"I just want you to lie there," she said between kisses, her voice more like a growl. She dragged her body along his, the movement dislodging the teddy. She freed her arms but let the garment drape from her waist—and then she made love to him.

She offered herself with such purity, it staggered him. Passion and openness, tantalizing touches of her hands and tongue and lips and teeth. The feel of her breath singeing his skin. The scrape of her fingernails along his inner thighs, then gliding higher. Her mouth caressing him, tentatively, then with explicit intent.

He groaned her name.

"You are power in a human form," she said, moving up his body. "Power and energy and vitality. Life." Her hands settled beside his head as she straddled him, her breasts close enough to taste. Her gaze unwaveringly on his, she freed the snaps holding the garment together between her legs, then she took him inside her leisurely, exquisitely. She asked for. He gave. She watched. He couldn't bear to. She freed something inside of him no one ever had. He couldn't stop her from stealing it, couldn't grab it back. She locked it beyond his reach, then she followed him into the same deep pool of oblivion until he pushed to the surface, gasping for air, the black layer of his soul now in her possession, and a new one unearthed in its place. He could feel the glow, painful in its intensity.

He kissed her, desperate to reclaim the man he'd always known. That man was gone, held prisoner inside her. He didn't know the one she'd liberated in its place. The one who pitied a broken old man. The one who'd fallen in love with the right woman at a time that couldn't have been more wrong.

He didn't know if she loved him, but she must believe it or she wouldn't have slept with him, he knew that much about her. He wanted to tell her. He wanted to hear the words himself in return.

Neither could happen.

She nuzzled him, purring her satisfaction, then she stretched like a cat coming awake from a nap in the sunshine. She landed on her side. He turned toward her, letting their legs entwine.

"It just gets better," she said, her eyes smiling, her hair tousled wildly around her face.

He tucked the silken strands behind her ears. "You humble me."

"Do I?" She snuggled into the pillow. "How?"

"You are a virtuous woman, *bella*. Do you know how rare that is?"

"How rare is it?"

"There is no punch line. I don't think I was ever as pure-hearted as you. Not even when I was a child."

"You have an interesting heart, Gabriel. I think you assign areas of it to certain people and things. You don't open it up all the way and let everyone and everything into it at once, though."

He stared at her as he analyzed her observation. He'd always compartmentalized his life. But could he do the same with emotions?

"You're looking much too serious," she said, sitting up. "I don't know about you but I didn't have much of an appetite today. Now I'm famished. Let's order some take-out."

By the time the doorbell rang, Cristina had slipped into a terry cloth bathrobe and Gabe wore his slacks again. He pulled his wallet from his back pocket as he walked to the door and opened it.

Jason Grimes stared back.

Fourteen

Cristina watched in shock as Jason pushed his way past Gabe and came uninvited into her apartment. She drew her robe more tightly against her, retying the sash as if strapping on armor. The door shut with a thud. Gabe sauntered up beside her as she and Jason squared off.

"Get the hell out of here, Marquez. This is between Cris and me."

"Is that what you want, *bella?*"

Oh, God. Gabe was being territorial, his endearment seeming almost more intimate than their state of undress. She shook her head, then found comfort in the strong hand he placed low on her back, possessive and soothing.

"Jason—"

"Don't, Cris. Don't say you're sorry. We know each other too well for that."

"I have nothing to apologize for. We don't have a relationship. I'm not cheating on you."

"You know how I feel," he said, his voice hoarse. "You know I've been working up to asking you to marry me."

"No, I don't know that. We're friends. Good friends."

"We have everything in common, Cris. It would be a good match. Our parents are expecting it."

"I don't love you."

He jerked back. His gaze shifted to Gabe for a second, then back to Cristina.

"Him? You love *him*, Cris? Or is he just keeping your bed warm? Give me a chance. I can be just as—"

"Stop! I'm sorry that you're hurting, but you have no right to intrude. My relationship with Gabe is private. I think you should go now."

"You don't know what you're doing." Jason reached for her hand. "He's going to destroy you. And your father won't permit this relationship to continue."

"My father doesn't make my decisions. Go, Jason. There's nothing else to say."

"There's plenty to say, but not here. Not now. This is far from over."

Gabe looked again for similarities between him and Jason Grimes—anything to declare them half brothers—but he saw nothing. He had a certain amount of compassion for the man. He had to go home and face his father in defeat, after all. But Jason had also enjoyed a father's attention all his life. Gabe resented that more than anything.

Jason stabbed at Gabe's chest with his forefinger. Gabe's first instinct was to knock his arm away. He resisted, standing still and silent instead, making him seem like a schoolyard bully as Gabe stared him down.

"We're not through, either, Marquez."

"The lady has made her choice."

"We'll see about that."

He slammed the door behind him.

"Well," Cristina said after a minute. "That was awkward, wasn't it?"

Gabe looked at her. A hint of a smile flickered across her lips without reaching her eyes.

"Don't look so surprised, Gabriel. I'm relieved, actually. I've been trying to let him down gently. I guess he just had to see for himself." She walked away, rubbing her arms. "I suppose he'll report to Father now. You know, I'm getting pretty tired of the men in my life trying to decide what's best for me."

"Why is your father in a wheelchair?"

She turned around, surprise lifting her brows. "He can walk, but it wears him out. He just doesn't have the strength he used to have. Why?"

"I thought perhaps he was ill."

"Not that I know of. And I'm pretty sure he'd tell me if he was. Anything to keep me at home."

Gabe moved toward her. "Do you have family besides him?"

"Distant cousins I haven't seen in years and years."

"So when your father dies, you won't have anyone."

He watched her swallow, then toss her hair behind her shoulders, her chin coming up sharply.

"I expect to have him around for a long time yet."

Gabe wished he didn't know what he knew. Cancer. Inoperable. How long did her father have? *Would* he use his condition to convince her to do her duty, as he called it?

The doorbell rang again. The Chinese take-out delivery this time, a welcome distraction.

They ate sprawled across her bed, ignored the phone that rang every hour, turned down the volume on the answering machine so that she didn't have to listen to her father's pleas to call him. Instead, she sketched Gabe sketching her. They laughed and talked and shared memories and made love. Then sometime around two o'clock in the morning, with his arms wrapped around her and his chest a pillow for her head, he fell asleep.

He dreamed that he lost her. That she hated him. That she walked down the aisle of a huge church, her gown a gossamer cloud that trailed her forever, to join Jason at the altar. Sebastian performed the marriage ceremony. Her father danced. Jason lifted her veil, bent to kiss her—

Gabe jerked awake. Sweat beading his forehead, he drew a

few long, slow breaths. Cristina shifted and sighed as he tightened his hold on her. He didn't have prophetic dreams, yet this one struck terror in him. She'd looked like the portrait he'd done before he knew her. She'd lost so much weight, her ribs were visible. And a tear trailed her cheek. She had sacrificed herself.

"Do you know I've never slept with anyone before?" she said into the dark and awful silence of the night. She stroked his skin idly.

"Neither have I."

"Were you dreaming?"

"Yes. I'm sorry I woke you."

"I don't mind. This feels good, just lying here with you." She paused. "Will you be able to go back to sleep?"

He heard the unasked question and answered it promptly. "I'm not going anywhere, *bella*." Although he undoubtedly wouldn't sleep again. Dawn was but an hour away, and he had too much to think about. "Go back to sleep."

"Hmm." She yawned, then settled. Soon she went limp against him.

He ran scenarios through his head, trying to find a solution that would be right for everyone. No one idea solved every problem. And at gut level he knew that Cristina stood little chance of escaping any situation pain free, whether he caused it or her father or Grimes.

How cavalier he'd been, believing that a little heartbreak would be unavoidable. How had he phrased it to himself? Something bearable. Something memorable. Even educational. She wouldn't be so gullible again.

He'd proved himself right, after all.

The sunny morning did nothing to ease Gabe's premonition of disaster. He left Cristina's apartment as soon as he could manage a smooth exit and drove home without once reaching the speed limit. If it had been possible, he would have moved away during the night. Started over. Created a whole new identity. And he would have taken Cristina with him.

Something waited for him at home. He felt it. Knew it. Dreaded it.

He shouldn't have left Cristina alone, either, but he couldn't be in two places at once.

The premonition took human form. Richard Grimes awaited him. Gabe saw him from the street, but took his time parking, then walked to the front door where Grimes stood.

"So it *is* you. I was hoping it wasn't the same Gabriel Marquez," the large, barrel-chested man said.

"One and the same, as you can see," Gabe replied, unlocking the door and inviting him in. He wanted him to see how he lived. How successful he was. How far he'd brought himself from the old neighborhood.

He climbed the magnificent staircase, letting Grimes follow. They would have their confrontation in his office, his domain, his kingdom. Gesturing to a chair, he seated himself behind his desk and assumed a casual pose, leaning back and rocking, watching as Grimes didn't sit but wandered around the room instead. He stopped in front of the De La Hoya portrait of his mother.

"You've done well for yourself."

"Yes, I have." *No thanks to you.*

He touched the frame. "Is your mother still as beautiful?"

"Even more so."

"I was sorry to give her up. My wife found out about her, you see, and gave me an ultimatum."

Gabe said nothing.

"I was more than a little surprised when you returned my money."

"With interest."

A slight smile. "Yes, of course." He took a seat opposite Gabe finally. "Arthur tells me you're quite a businessman."

"I could own you, if I wanted," Gabe said without inflection.

"Could you?"

"Yes." He watched his father shift in his chair.

"Is that your goal?"

"Perhaps."

"And your plans for Cristina?"

"Are none of your business." It was easier than he thought, Gabe realized. He'd wanted this confrontation for so long, and now it was happening. He felt strong. Invincible. Powerful.

"It's important that my son marry Arthur's daughter."

His son. Gabe linked his fingers over his stomach. "Is it?"

"There has been an understanding."

"Someone should tell Cristina that."

Grimes had the grace to look away, his cheeks flushing. "She needed to sow some wild oats first. We decided to give her time."

So he'd been reduced to being classified as wild oats and not a serious threat to the success of their plan. "Did you?"

His lips compressed. "I'm here to see if we can reach some accord about the situation."

"I'm listening."

"I was prepared to offer you money, but you say you have no need of it. Perhaps I can tempt you with something else."

Gabe waited.

Grimes leaned forward. "For all your skill with finances, you've never held a position of power. I can put you on the board of directors of several corporations. Or find you a presidency of a powerhouse company. The perks would astound you. Travel. Luxury. Women."

"I thought you were going to tempt me."

Grimes sat back, his jaw twitching. "I can't believe there's nothing you want or need. At some point in his life, every man desires something he can't seem to get on his own."

"I haven't reached that point." Gabe snagged a letter opener from his desktop. He pressed the tip into his palm as he eyed the man across from him, the man who was quickly losing the veneer of civility he'd worn until now. "But perhaps there's something I can do for you, instead."

"I doubt that."

"Perhaps I spoke too soon. It isn't what *I* can do for you, but what my friend could."

"Your friend?"

Gabe's tone of voice must have alerted him. He went rigid.

"My very good friend, Sebastian Blackstone."

Grimes shot out of the chair, then lurched over the desk, his fists clenched. Color rose in his face, a vivid wash of mottled red. Gabe looked at him with mild interest.

"You! I knew someone was digging. You'll find nothing, you know. Nothing at all."

"Then why are you upset?"

"I don't like being toyed with."

Gabe pushed back his chair and stood. "Neither do I. Neither did my mother."

"I took good care of your mother. I didn't have to, but I did. I paid her well when I left."

"And what does that make her?"

A lead blanket of silence descended.

Grimes headed for the door. "We're not finished. Not by a long shot."

The front door slammed as he left. Like father, like son.

Like father, like son. The words sat there for a while in Gabe's mind. He hadn't felt a familial connection to Richard Grimes—not before, and certainly not now. That old link, and the even older curiosity, was broken at last. Gabe had faced him as an adult—and won. He felt sorry for his half brother, who was also a victim, but Gabe had no intention of telling Jason about their relationship, either. One innocent had already been hurt, and Gabe wouldn't add to that. But he needed to lay his past to rest, for his own peace of mind. Now he could deal with the future.

He sank into his chair and picked up the phone. His hand shook as he dialed Cristina's number.

After reaching her answering machine he hung up, setting the receiver carefully in the cradle. He rubbed his face with his hands, then let his arms drop to the desktop.

She'd been ordered home. He had no doubt of it.

Now he waited.

Cristina clenched the drapes. She didn't feel the sun beating down on her through the window of her father's solarium. Her bones were so cold that her flesh felt like ice.

"So, Father, the bottom line is that the building that Richard's company was constructing collapsed. A worker was paralyzed in the accident, a man who says it fell because too many corners were cut."

"He claims that the materials used were substantially below acceptable quality than what was bid and approved."

Cristina turned around and studied her father. "As I recall from the newspaper accounts, there was some movement of the earth, so the speculation was that it wasn't being constructed at the current level of requirements for earthquake safety. That would seem to place fault not only on materials but also on method and maybe even inspections."

He looked away.

"Where is the man who got hurt, Father? *Can* he prove it?"

"He disappeared. Convenient, isn't it?"

Fear crawled down her back at his too-blasé tone of voice. "Exactly how are you involved?"

He tucked his hands close to him. "I needed money. Richard needed someone who could get him this job. We made a trade."

"Your political pull for cash."

"Yes."

"That's not unusual, is it? Isn't that what the good ol' boys network is all about? I know how far your sphere of influence extends."

"Think this through, daughter. Criminal charges haven't been filed, but when—if—this man does come back with the proof he says he has, Richard could go to jail. I called in every favor owed me in the business community."

"You made an honest mistake."

The lines on his face deepened. "My credibility would be completely gone. Everything I worked for all these years, all the good I did, would be lost. I want to die with dignity, Cristina—and with the respect I earned. I want my place in history."

She crouched before him and covered his hands with hers.

"It's Richard's problem. You didn't know what he was doing."

A long pause followed, then, "I did. God help me, I did. Not in the beginning, but perhaps in time to change things."

Cristina's heart slammed painfully against her ribs. Her fingers dug into her father's frail hands. "No."

The air turned electric.

"No, I don't believe that."

"For God's sake, child, the only reason I was able to avoid filing for bankruptcy was Richard's generosity. The only way I can prevent it now is if you marry Jason. We have to show a united front. We have to appear as if nothing is wrong. And I need Richard's money."

She stood, her legs shaking.

He pressed on with his argument. "With my name and Richard's financial backing, we'd be untouchable, no matter what that injured man says. He wouldn't stand a chance."

Shattered, she took a few steps back. One thing she'd thought she could count on was her father's honesty.

"So you want me to be the sacrifice, Father, is that it?" Sacrifice. The word stopped her cold for a minute, then she shoved it aside, although a hazy picture of Gabe's haunting portrait lingered in her mind.

"Sacrifice? You've always liked Jason. You had a crush on him. I wouldn't consign you to a lifetime with someone you couldn't abide."

"A crush? Father, that was ten years ago! He offered to take me to the prom when no one else did. I was grateful. You can't confuse that with an emotional commitment strong enough for marriage."

His eyes pleaded with her. "I won't live forever, Cristina. I have to know you'll be taken care of. I have to know my name won't be tarnished. This is important to me."

"So important that I have to marry someone I don't love? The son of a criminal? You want me to be part of *that* family?"

Her father started to speak, but another masculine voice answered.

"That hasn't been proven."

Cristina spun around at the intrusion. Richard Grimes stood in the doorway.

"Nor will it be," he continued, coming into the room. "If Sebastian Blackstone actually did have incriminating evidence, he would have come forward long before now. He's just trying to shift blame."

"Sebastian...?" Cristina's mind went blank first, then got crowded with suspicion that flowed straight to her heart. Sebastian? A coincidence. Surely it had to be a coincidence.

"Blackstone," Grimes said, completing the name. "I believe you're acquainted with his very good friend, Gabriel Marquez."

Her father swore, which confused her more than ever. She had never known him to swear.

She made her way to a chair, reached blindly for the arms, then lowered herself slowly down. She heard the words the men exchanged, repulsive conclusions about Gabe's deliberate seduction of Cristina, the purpose of which they could only speculate about, but which seemed obvious. The tentacles of Gabe's business contacts reached far and wide, apparently. He wanted to hurt those who had hurt his friend. He couldn't find enough to target her father or Richard directly, so Cristina became an alternate target. Get to them through her. Just from their first contact Gabe would have determined that she was a woman desperate for attention.

It made sense. And yet...he'd cared about her, really cared. He couldn't have faked that. Could he?

She had to sort out what she knew from what they were guessing. She had to force the pain gathering like a fireball inside her to stay away until she knew for sure. He wouldn't have lied to her like that. He wouldn't have. She couldn't be that wrong. He'd touched her with such tenderness. Kissed her with such desire. Made love to her with such need. He slept with her! Slept the whole night in her bed—breaking his own rule. He'd shared his worst memories—or had he made them up in order to draw out hers? Why?

God. She had to know.

She didn't want to know.

She'd survived humiliation before. But this time—

"I'm leaving," she said, standing.

"Cristina," her father said. "If you don't marry Jason, there will be nothing left for you. He wants to marry you. He'll provide for you and protect you."

"I can take care of myself."

"If my reputation is shattered, you'll lose most of your clients. You'll need a husband."

Closing her eyes against his assumption, she tried to remember that he was a product of his generation as much as she was of hers. "Not one I don't love," she said quietly. "And if this Sebastian Blackstone does have proof, my marrying Jason wouldn't make a bit of difference, would it?"

"You'd be surprised," Richard Grimes said. "We believe we can disprove anything the man says. Anything."

"Because you can afford to pay to circumvent the truth."

Grimes smiled. "Reasonable doubt, Cristina. I realize you're a little upset at the moment. Having Marquez use you like that has to be extremely painful. Especially for you."

"Why especially for me?"

"Well, you're not exactly used to men beating down your door, are you?"

"Shut up, Richard." Her father's voice resounded with command; he expected automatic compliance.

Cristina lifted her chin. She would not take a step back, not when she'd come so far. She wouldn't let them destroy what she accepted. She was worthy of being loved. She was a beautiful, desirable woman. Gabe said so. Gabe said.

Gabe.

She hurried from the house. She knew where she had to go and who she had to see now.

The truth couldn't wait.

Fifteen

From his studio window, he watched her slam her car door and run up the walkway. He didn't doubt why she was there.

Counting off the seconds, Gabe waited, following her progress by sounds—a few words exchanged with his housekeeper. The front door shutting. Hurried footsteps up the first staircase. The second. Across the landing. Then she burst through the door and came to a halt.

He didn't move from his post by the window. He watched and waited. The truth wasn't an ally now, but his most bitter enemy. He would give her the truth, however, because he owed her that much. He didn't deserve to be heard, to explain why, to be forgiven. What he'd done to her was an obscenity against decency. The payback would be—should be—brutal.

"Did you maneuver our meeting at the gallery?" she asked directly, not coming any farther into the room.

"Yes."

The tiny flicker of hope in her face died a sudden death. Her lips trembled.

"Did you set out to seduce me?"

"Yes."

She pressed her hand to her mouth. A curtain of reaction fell over her eyes—hurt, disbelief, disillusion.

She dropped her hand, pushed back her shoulders and lifted her chin. "Were you seeking revenge for Sebastian?"

"I was buying him time."

"By seducing me."

"By preventing a marriage between you and Jason Grimes."

"By seducing me," she stated flatly. "How did you know about it? I didn't even know."

"I made it my business."

"You used me."

He didn't defend the accusation that pierced his heart then ripped clear through his soul. He bled—she just couldn't see it.

"You toyed with me. You violated the trust I gave you."

Again he couldn't deny her words.

She took a step toward him, then stopped.

"I shared my secrets," she said, the words barely more than a whisper. "I shared my body. I shared my heart, Gabriel. My *heart*. And you never wanted any of it."

How wrong she was. Her heart mattered most. He'd found that out too late. She'd stolen the darkness that had clung to his soul for all these years, and now it was poisoning her instead. If he could find a way to take it back, he would.

"Congratulations. You really had me believing you." She moved toward the canvas he'd been working on. "I want to see my portrait before I go."

Gabe made a move to stop her. It was the wrong canvas. The wrong one—

She gasped. Her hands flew to her mouth. "Oh, God. Oh, God! How could you? *How could you?*"

"Cristina—"

"I didn't pose for this! I never would have posed nude. Never. Not even for you."

"I painted you from memory." The blessing and curse of

a photographic memory. He lifted the cloth covering her official portrait. "This is for you. That was for me."

Panic cast a brilliant sheen over her eyes.

"So this next step was blackmail? Or perhaps a little routine public humiliation? What? *Why?*"

He moved toward her. "It never would have gone on display. I promise you that. But I couldn't help painting it."

"You *promise?* Oh, well, let me take that one to the bank, along with all the flattery, all the lies about how beautiful I am. And desirable. I'm surprised you could even get it up. Oh, that's right. Sex is just basic to you, isn't it? One woman's as good as the next. I was pathetically easy, wasn't I? God. I look like some porn star."

The crudeness of her words showed him exactly how much he'd hurt her. "It wasn't flattery. Nor lies. You have to believe that much." But why should she believe him? Actions spoke louder than words. "And there's nothing pornographic about this. The sheets cover most of you."

"I look like a tramp."

"No." He knew he was arguing without any chance of getting through to her. He wanted to hold her. To tell her he loved her. To ask her—

"I will never forgive you for this."

She looked past him, then calmly strode across the room. He saw a flash of something in her hand as she turned around. A heartbeat later she stabbed the unfinished portrait with a paint trowel and dragged it through the canvas, splitting herself asunder. Then she moved to the portrait destined for the Chandler family gallery and destroyed it as well. He didn't try to stop her, although he died with the work. The best work of his life.

She flung the trowel aside, the clatter of metal a ringing accusation. Eyes blazing, she marched up to him.

"I won't beg for mercy for my father. Because he was desperate, he got caught up in something he's sorry happened. He also has no control over it now. You probably won't believe this, but he's been an honorable man most of his life. When my mother died, he lost interest in living. His finances dwindled. He didn't realize it until it was too late. Then he did something stupid. For me, Gabriel. For *me*. Are you so perfect that you've never done anything stupid?''

He wanted to soothe the pain from her face, to beg her forgiveness, to promise her the moon.

She walked away, then turned around when she reached the door. ''I wouldn't have married Jason, no matter what ammunition my father used. And you know what? I thought you were the first man to see how strong I could be. To have faith in that strength. I thought you were different. Even exceptional.''

''I'm sorry, Cristina.''

Her eyes welled, the tears glittering but not spilling out. She tossed back her hair and drew herself up proudly.

''I'm willing to take some of the blame. I was drawn to the uncivilized side of you, to the dangerous edge that made me burn. I thought you were the best thing to ever happen to me— no matter what the final outcome was. You accepted me. No one else ever had, not without qualification. But now I realize I was wrong. *I* would have been the best thing that ever happened to *you*. You never deserved me—but you could've had me for life.''

What could he say to the truth?

''You were right about one thing, Gabriel. There's a fine line between love and hate—and you crossed it. I hate you.''

Even her parting words didn't blacken his soul. She'd taken that from him and not given it back. He wanted it back, that retreat from the world of hopes and dreams that most people lived in. He wanted the familiar darkness to surround him and bring the old peace that came with the satisfaction of winning. Instead she left all her goodness shining on him in painful rays, and all her hopes and dreams entrusted to him. How could he give them back to her? How could he steal back his bitter soul, his untouched heart, and leave hers free to love again?

Hearing an engine rev, he moved to the window in time to see her car speed away. He traced the panes of glass with his fingers, watching the streaks he left, his mind filled with visions of her standing there, a sea captain's devoted wife, her eyes shimmering with tenderness and warmth.

But not for him.

"Take care of yourself, *bella*," he whispered, his breath fogging the glass, his heart hurting.

He found a roll of tape. His hands shaking, he reverently taped the canvases back together, the only tangible evidence that something pure had touched him once.

He'd come to her untainted by his past. She didn't know that. *He* hadn't known it. The first time they'd made love had been his first time—in love. There was a difference. Another thing he'd been wrong about. It was different with a woman you love. More joyous, more precious, more satisfying.

And she'd loved him. The unworthy, undeserving man he was. She'd loved him.

His paintbrush might as well have been a sword.

"Gabriel?"

He spun toward the quiet voice, hopeful. Not Cristina. How foolish to think it would be Cristina.

"Mom."

He tried to pull himself together. He couldn't even walk across the room to greet her—and yet what he wanted was to be held, as she used to hold him when he was a child.

He jammed his hands in his front pockets. "What are you doing here?"

"Richard came to see me."

Bewilderment lined her face, so beautiful, even at fifty. Her hair was fashioned into an intricate twist, but Gabe knew it reached her waist in a shining ebony cascade, not a strand of gray visible yet. Her body was a little softer these days, but it only added to her elegant grace.

"*Hijo*, he said you threatened him."

Gabe swiped a hand down his face. He invited his mother to sit in Cristina's chair—he would always think of it as that— then he pulled the ottoman close. "I didn't threaten him. He did something criminal, and he deserves to be punished, but if he's feeling threatened it's because his own conscience is talking to him."

"I had not seen him since he left, all those years ago. He looks almost the same."

Gabe stiffened. "Don't tell me you still love him."

She smiled slightly. "No. What I felt for Richard disappeared long ago. Even then, I would not have named it love. I had an affection for him. And I was grateful. I have told you many, many times, *hijo,* I loved your father. I would have died for your father. No one can replace him in my heart."

Gabe's world tilted. "My father? But my father is Richard Grimes. And you just said—"

"Richard? No, no, no!"

She laid a hand upon Gabe's arm just as his head began to spin.

"I told you, Gabriel. I told you hundreds of times. You are descended from kings! How could Richard Grimes be a king?"

"But...you worked in Grimes's house. He got you pregnant."

"I was pregnant when he hired me as a maid. I had just come to this country from Mexico. I never said he was your father, *hijo.* After you were born, he moved me into the house where you grew up."

"Why would I have assumed it?" He ran his hands through his hair. His world was crashing down around him. "You said my father was a strong and powerful man. Grimes came every week to see you. He paid your bills."

"He provided the house and sometimes more. But I worked cleaning houses. I took little from Richard."

"He paid you off when he left! He paid *me* off!"

"He was my lover, *sí,* to my shame. I did not know for many, many years that he married, but by then I did not think I had a choice. Your father, Ramón, sent me here when we learned I carried his child. I had nothing. He was to join us, but he was killed before he could."

"Why didn't you tell me this?" Gabe lurched upright, shouting the words. Everything he was, everything he'd done had been born out of his hatred for Richard Grimes.

"Because it was dangerous, *hijo*. Your father was a powerful man. *Un revolucionario.*"

"Why didn't you go home? Why didn't you tell his family about me? Wouldn't they have protected you? Cared for you? Helped you raise me?"

"You would have become a—how do you say, *empeño?*"

"A pawn. *Madre,* I have been a man for a long, long time. You should have told me this. You should have told me."

She flew out of the chair and grabbed his arms, putting a stop to his prowling.

"I told you all your life! Your name is Gabriel Alejandro De La Hoya y Marquez, and you are descended from kings! *Es verdad.* Truth. I can show you on paper the line from which you come. It is an old and noble name, *hijo.*"

"You knew I thought he was my father. You knew it."

She seemed to age before his eyes. "Perhaps I should have told you more. But you did not ask specifically. And after Richard left us, you never wanted to discuss your father, and I was grateful. Because I was afraid."

"Afraid of what?"

She choked out the words. "That you would take your father's place. That you would die for his cause. You are all I have, Gabriel. All I have. I had given up the only other thing I loved. I could not give you up, too."

"I wouldn't have gone to take his place."

"*Sí, mi hijo,* you would. You are a strong man. A man of great loyalty. You would have sought your roots. You would have taken your father's place. I know you. I know you too well."

"So you intentionally kept my heritage from me, because it was easier and it suited your need to keep me close?"

"I did not want to lose you."

Instead, he'd lost himself somewhere along the way. There was nothing for him to hold on to. He'd dug his own path, shovelful by shovelful. "Why didn't you let yourself love another man? An honest man? One who would have been a father to me and a true husband to you. You deserved that. So did I."

"If you can say that, *hijo,* you have never loved. Not the kind of love that you carry in your heart for all your days."

"Sometimes second best is enough, *Madre.*"

"You would say such a thing? Second best would never be good enough for you."

"Maybe I would have been a different person if I'd had a father around to talk to. A better person."

"Lo siento, hijo. Lo siento."

She was sorry. What more did he expect from her? They couldn't turn back the clock.

He's not my father. The words he'd wished for all his life had come true—too late. So many people had been hurt because of his anger. Maybe he couldn't ever forgive himself, but he could forgive his mother. She'd suffered enough.

"I'm sorry, too, Mom." He wrapped his arms around her, his misguided mother who had done her best.

As Arthur Chandler had. But instead of blaming her father, Cristina felt compassion for him. Love. And she let that rule her decisions. Gabe could do the same.

Long after his mother left, he sat staring at the damaged portraits. He heard his housekeeper call out that she was leaving, but he didn't answer her. He was glad to be alone, even though he didn't know what to do next.

He'd always known what to do next.

"You didn't call me."

Gabe spun around at the sound of the harsh masculine voice. Ben. Great. Just what he needed.

"Remind me to have the locks changed." He stood abruptly and moved away from the portraits, not wanting Ben to see them. "I had Raymond take down the painting at the gallery."

"I saw. We still have business to discuss, Gabe. You had no right to put us on display like that."

Ben had picked the wrong time for a confrontation. If he wanted a fight, he'd come to the right place.

"You're an idiot," Gabe said. He watched Ben's reaction settle, then build, until his fists clenched and his body turned to steel.

"I'm tired of you telling me how to live my life. You don't know anything," Ben said in a deceptively soft voice.

"I know a lot. I know I would give up everything I have for what you threw away. Damn it, Ben. You had a woman who loved you. Only you. Who would've been by your side until death."

"You always take Les's side."

The accusation stung—because it was true and because Ben's pain accompanied the words. "You've been jealous of me since the first day we all met, just because I flirted with her. She rejected me, Ben! And the minute she saw you, that was it. She never looked at another man."

"You wanted her."

"She was cute. I flirted. It was habit."

Ben turned away. "You've been her confidant."

"I've been her friend. That's all."

"You're supposed to be my friend, too."

The words hung in the air between them. God, why was everything happening to him at the same time?

"Gabriel Marquez, the perfect man," Ben said, facing Gabe again. "The man with all the money. All the women—"

"And look where it got me. Do I look happy to you? Do you see a special woman?" He gestured violently around him. "A child? The proverbial white picket fence?"

"Is that what you want?"

The question brought Gabe up short. They didn't ask these kinds of questions of each other. "Yes," he said at last. His throat burned. He sank into a chair and buried his head in his hands. "God, yes."

After a long silence he felt a hand come to rest on his shoulder. "Do you want to talk about it?"

No! The word echoed in his mind. He sensed Ben crouching beside him.

"I'll listen. Maybe we can start our friendship over, Gabe. I'm willing to try, anyway. I'm tired of being at odds with you."

"Then can we get drunk together, because that's what I plan on doing, and I'd rather not do it alone."

"I imagine you can convince me."

Gabe smiled slightly. Maybe something good would come out of the disaster he'd made of his life, after all, if he could straighten things out with Ben. "I guess you'd better pull up a chair, then. This won't be short or sweet."

Sixteen

"Gabriel Marquez did not pay off your debts as any kind of favor to me!" Cristina shouted at her father. "He was easing his own guilty conscience, that's all. Now look what you've done! Saddled me with an even bigger debt because I'll owe *him*. How could you?"

"Calm down, Cristina."

"I will not calm down. And stop giving me the pathetic invalid look. Your mind isn't the least bit frail." She dropped into the seat beside her father's bed, a chair she'd occupied for most of the past week since she'd moved home. She owed Gabe a debt of gratitude for convincing her father to tell her about his illness, but the guilt scales tipped too heavily on Gabe's side to worry about showing him her appreciation. "I can't believe you took money from him," she said, dragging her hands down her face.

"He had reasons I couldn't argue with, my dear. Besides which, my life insurance will cover most of the reimbursement, so you won't be beholden to him." He patted Cristina's arm. "He promised he'd do everything he could to keep my name out of the investigation into the building collapse, said I seemed to be an innocent party." He looked away a moment. "We both know I wasn't. Richard used me, but I allowed it. And he'll drag me down with him, especially now that his plans for the marriage have been shattered. With any luck, I'll die before anything goes to trial."

"Oh, Father, don't say that. Please don't." She leaned across to hug him. "Let's just cherish this time."

"The practicalities need to be dealt with. Did you know Gabe's mother was Richard's mistress for almost sixteen years?"

Cristina straightened. "What?"

"It's true. Richard told me after you left here the other day. Since Gabe was an infant, apparently."

Sixteen years? But his father had taken him to the call girl on his fifteenth birthday. His father.

His father was Richard Grimes?

"I think your Mr. Marquez is a complicated man, Cristina. True to his beliefs, right or wrong. Perhaps a little unyielding, but someone you could count on."

Still stunned by the revelation, she didn't comprehend her father's words immediately. "Wait. You *want* me to be involved with Gabe?"

"He's nothing like Jason, is he? Jason wouldn't have the guts to stand up to me. Your Gabriel may not be an angel, but he would protect you. I admire him. And he did make you happy for a while. Happier than I've ever seen you."

"But, Father, I'd never trust him. What's a relationship without trust? And what makes you think he even wants a relationship with me?" *He hasn't even tried to contact me.*

"Miss Cristina?"

Welcoming the interruption, she turned to the man hovering in the doorway, one of only three servants left in the Chandler employ.

"A package arrived for you. I had the delivery man put it in your studio. Looks to be some artwork."

"Just one package? There should be several boxes. My computer, as well as the paintings from my apartment."

"Just the one crate, miss."

"Hmm. Thank you, John." She turned to her father, but he'd drifted to sleep. She fought the sting of tears at seeing him so fragile. In the week she'd been home they'd become closer than ever, more open. More loving. It was hard watching him die, watching his pain take over, but she was grateful to be with him.

Cristina turned off the bedside lamp then went to her studio. They would finish their discussion about Gabe later.

Gabe. How could she have been so wrong about him? Oh, she'd seen and acknowledged his flaws, but she hadn't detected a hint of malice toward her. Speculation, curiosity, interest. Never malice. Yet only a man with hate in his heart could have used her like that, without thought to how it would devastate her. How could he have missed seeing the love she offered him?

With a groan, she put her hands over her ears, as if it would block her thoughts. Giving herself something to do, she opened the crate.

A sheet of parchment fell to the ground, landing on her feet. When she saw the signature, the paper imprisoned her as if it weighed a ton. She didn't want to read any lies he wrote, but as she shifted her glance to the open crate, she saw the painting of her nude. He'd taped it together, leaving it unfinished and unframed. Behind it was her De La Hoya original for the family gallery. He'd redone it. Framed it. Sent it to her.

And she looked beautiful.

She hadn't seen beyond paint and canvas last week in his studio. She'd only wanted to destroy it, the way he had destroyed her dreams and her trust.

Cristina let the first canvas fall facedown on the floor, then she propped the masterpiece on an easel. The note he'd written tempted her. She ignored it for as long as she could. If it had been in an envelope, she would have torn it to shreds. But then, he probably knew that about her.

Crouching, she picked up the paper with her fingertips.

This was the only way I could show you the truth.

Gabe

Cristina threw the paper as far as it would go—about a foot. It drifted to the floor and lay there like a death sentence.

Show her the truth? What truth?

He didn't do anything without a purpose, but exactly what was he saying? Why was he making a game of it, making her guess at the meaning behind his words?

Show her what truth?

She'd learned something important since she'd met him—that the truth wasn't a straight path, as she'd always thought, but one that wove around problems and burrowed through disappointments. So, what hid in the portraits?

Hard truths like the one Gabe lived with—the knowledge that Richard Grimes was his father, a father who wouldn't acknowledge him? She pictured Gabe at fifteen, so full of anticipation, only to be so cruelly abandoned.

She said his name on a sigh full of sadness for him.

Her movements stiff, she swept up the portrait she'd left facedown and propped it against the easel legs, below the other, then examined both paintings for the meaning behind his note.

Everything she admired about his work was evident—and something extra, as well. Maybe because she was the subject, and she wanted to believe he felt differently about her than about anyone else he'd painted, she also saw a tone unlike any she'd seen in his previous work, a loving tone. The work was sensual—and tasteful—but love made her eyes shimmer and the corners of her mouth curve.

As she stared at his portraits, tension flowed from her, like a willow tree straightening again after a long, steady wind had kept it bent. She'd been strong before she knew him. Now she was stronger. She'd gone past accepting herself to even liking the way she looked.

He'd broken down every one of her barriers. Could she give that up? Could she forgive him?

Could she trust a man whose nickname was Romeo? His talent was in making a woman feel good about herself.

Then the critical question—was he even asking her forgiveness, or was she fantasizing about that, too?

She had to find out.

She recognized the music instantly. Wagner. Played loud enough that paintings bounced against the walls, tilting crazily.

Cristina thanked the housekeeper, then climbed the stairway, taking tentative steps toward the blaring notes. He wouldn't have heard her if she'd jogged, but she tiptoed, anyway, stalling. She didn't know if she could face another disappointment from him.

She stopped just inside the doorway, catching her breath at the sight of him. Wearing only jeans, he painted on a huge canvas, something in response to the music. A landscape of his soul, it seemed, in a blast of color, like a heart exploding. She watched the play of muscles along his back and shoulders. Even his bare feet mesmerized her. No longer a cool, controlled man, but one overflowing with emotion, as if everything held in reserve had burst free at one time.

She moved until she could touch him, pressing her fingertips to his back, whispering his name into the musical explosion of brass and strings and drums that was deafening, tantalizing.

He spun around so fast she jumped. She'd sliced into his concentration when she touched him. It took a few seconds for him to register her, for the wild passion in his eyes to calm.

"Cristina."

Just her name, but with such a wealth of emotion on his face that she forgot her questions. He set his palette and brush aside, then grabbed his shirt hanging over the screen and slipped into it.

"I would have been more presentable if you'd called first," he said after turning off the music, his gaze cool.

She studied his expression and decided he was shielding himself against being hurt.

"I got the paintings."

"Will you keep them?"

"One of them, at least."

His lips compressed, but he said nothing.

"I need to know what you meant by your note. What truth are you showing me, Gabe?"

"The truth of who you are."

"Who am I?"

They had stood like this once before, in almost the exact same spots, facing each other, neither moving, when he'd let her know he was also Alejandro De La Hoya. His trust had been such a gift then.

"Who are you?" he queried at last. "You're a much better person than I."

"Why don't you just lay your cards on the table, Gabriel? I have so many questions I don't know where to start."

He wiped a hand down his face, then through his already disheveled hair. It was the first time he hadn't looked neat. "You already said you wouldn't forgive me. What difference would anything I say make?"

"Maybe a lot."

Hope flared in his eyes then was doused with his next blink. Had no one ever given him a second chance before? The utter sadness of it made her want to weep.

"I never wanted to hurt you, Cristina. If you believe nothing else, believe that."

"You set me up from the beginning to be hurt."

He warded off the verbal blow with a subtle shifting of his shoulders. "I know it seems that way. In my misguided attempt to help Sebastian, I thought I might be saving you, as well, from a marriage that would be more of a merger. I didn't know your strength—because I didn't want to. I do now." He looked away. "In the end I'm no better than Richard Grimes. I used you, too. Believe me, I'm paying for it."

"How?"

"Because for all that I may have changed your life irrevocably, you've changed mine even more."

"Tell me how."

His mouth twisted. "I deserve this, I suppose."

"Deserve what?" Her legs were beginning to shake from standing still and taut for so long, but she couldn't move, either. Didn't want to walk toward or away from him. They just faced each other and dealt with it all.

"The ultimate revenge, right, Cristina? Revenge is one thing I do understand. Okay. You want the whole truth? Here it is. I've learned a hell of a lot about myself since we met. I've changed. You drained me of the envy and the hate I had for a man I thought had hurt my mother and me, then you left me with all this...*light* inside. I don't know what to do with it. I want the darkness back, *bella*. I need the darkness back or I'm going to lose my mind. I hurt—" He stopped, as if knowing he'd said too much.

A tangle of emotions flowed from him, filling the space between them like something palpable.

"Why did you pay my father's debts?"

He frowned, as if the answer was simple.

"So that you had choices. My God, Cristina. It's only money. What does it matter?"

"My pride matters."

"It was the only thing I could think of to pay you back for what I'd done to you." He swore. "You mean, I screwed that up, too? I just wanted to give you a clean slate. Your career will solve the rest."

"You're still going to show my work?"

"Of course I am." He shoved his hands through his hair again, swore again. "You don't trust me at all, do you?"

"Why does it matter?" she asked, her throat aching. "Why is it so important?"

His face reflected stark pain. "You're going to make me say the words."

"I have to," she whispered.

He moved so close she could feel the heat from his body, feel his breath dust her face, warm and unsteady.

"I love you," he said, his voice low and harsh, suffused with passion. "Beyond my own worthiness. Beyond all my dreams. Beyond life. If anyone had told me I could love like this—" He stopped. Swallowed.

Love poured from her like a hot spring forcing its way through an ice floe, melting her resistance, her hesitance, her doubts. He'd never known the safety and security she had. Maybe it was time he learned they weren't just words.

"I love you, too." Oh, the joy of being able to say the words aloud!

He breathed her name as he reached for her, tentatively at first, then almost painfully, pulling her close, holding her as if the world were coming to an end and this was the last time the second hand would sweep the clock.

"I don't deserve this," he said, as if she would disappear.

"Yes, you do. *We* do. I love you so much."

Gabe pulled her even closer. She loved him. He felt her fingers dig into his back, felt her shoulders shake—and the pieces of his broken world finally fit themselves together, the jagged edges melding to create one smooth sphere, with Cristina in the middle.

He stroked her spine, spoke against her hair, the words tumbling unchecked. "I've been alone much of my life, *bella,* but I'd never been truly lonely—not until you were gone from my life. I never thought I needed anyone. I thought I could take care of myself just fine, that I only needed the challenges I gave myself."

He pulled back enough to look into her eyes. Eyes brimming with love and joy.

"I was wrong. I need you. And a family. The whole fantasy of home that I never believed in before. Please marry me. You won't have a moment's doubt of my fidelity or my love. And I promise never to disappoint you again.''

''Shh.'' She pressed her fingers to his lips. ''You can't promise that. No relationship is that perfect. But on the way here I remembered something you said about marriage vows being the purest vows a man makes. I've seen for myself what loyalty means to you. I love you, Gabriel. With all my heart. Yes, I'd be honored to marry you.''

He tried to kiss her tenderly to show her how much her answer meant, but he had to expunge his fears first, his despair that he thought he'd lost her, his fury at himself that he'd hurt her. What the kiss lacked in tenderness, it made up for in honest need. Returning need poured from her, as well. She attacked him back, a fierce warrior goddess.

''If I don't have you naked against me in the next minute—'' he murmured against her mouth ''—I'm going to stop breathing.''

''I've learned mouth-to-mouth resuscitation.''

Her smile blinded him. He scooped her into his arms and carried her down a flight of stairs and into his bedroom, ignoring her little shrieks of fear that he was going to fall and break both their necks. Kicking the bedroom door shut behind them, he dropped her on his bed—their bed.

''I need a favor,'' she said, a little breathless as he unbuttoned her blouse.

''Anything.''

''I want to get married right away, before my father— Before.''

''Is Saturday soon enough? You already have the dress. I'll move into your house,'' he said, shifting his gaze to her face, seeing gratitude settle in her eyes. ''We'll care for him together.''

''Thank you,'' she said, a soft hitch in her voice.

''I'm going to be with you, *bella*. You can count on me. You won't bear any burdens alone.''

''Neither will you.''

''I have so much to tell you. About Sebastian and my father. Secrets and lies, Cristina. So many secrets and lies.''

She threaded her fingers through his hair over and over, her smile gentle and accepting. ''We have all the time in the world, my love.''

He laid his head against her breasts, enjoying the pillow of comfort, savoring the scent of her flesh—a privilege he would have for the rest of his life.

The rest of his life.

He smiled. And then he sought his mate.

* * * * *

Look for Ben and Leslie's story,
HIS ULTIMATE TEMPTATION,
coming in December from Silhouette Desire,
when THE LONE WOLVES series continues.

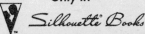

Take 2 bestselling love stories FREE

Plus get a FREE surprise gift!

Special Limited-Time Offer

Mail to Silhouette Reader Service™

3010 Walden Avenue
P.O. Box 1867
Buffalo, N.Y. 14240-1867

YES! Please send me 2 free Silhouette Desire® novels and my free surprise gift. Then send me 6 brand-new novels every month, which I will receive months before they appear in bookstores. Bill me at the low price of $3.12 each plus 25¢ delivery and applicable sales tax, if any.* That's the complete price, and a saving of over 10% off the cover prices—quite a bargain! I understand that accepting the books and gift places me under no obligation ever to buy any books. I can always return a shipment and cancel at any time. Even if I never buy another book from Silhouette, the 2 free books and the surprise gift are mine to keep forever.

225 SEN CH7U

Name	(PLEASE PRINT)	
Address	Apt. No.	
City	State	Zip

This offer is limited to one order per household and not valid to present Silhouette Desire® subscribers. *Terms and prices are subject to change without notice.
Sales tax applicable in N.Y.

UDES-98   ©1990 Harlequin Enterprises Limited

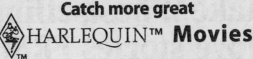

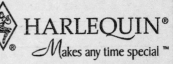

MATERNITY LEAVE

Coming September 1998

Three delightful stories about the blessings
and surprises of "Labor" Day.

TABLOID BABY by Candace Camp

She was whisked to the hospital in the nick of time....

THE NINE-MONTH KNIGHT
by Cait London

A down-on-her-luck secretary is experiencing
odd little midnight cravings....

THE PATERNITY TEST by Sherryl Woods

The stick turned blue before her
biological clock struck twelve....

*These three special women are very pregnant...and very
single, although they won't be either for too much longer,
because baby—and Daddy—are on their way!*

Available at your favorite retail outlet.

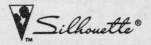

MEN at WORK

All work and no play?
Not these men!

July 1998
MACKENZIE'S LADY by Dallas Schulze

Undercover agent Mackenzie Donahue's
lazy smile and deep blue eyes were his best
weapons. But after rescuing—and kissing!—
damsel in distress Holly Reynolds, how could
he betray her by spying on her brother?

August 1998
MISS LIZ'S PASSION by Sherryl Woods

Todd Lewis could put up a building with ease,
but quailed at the sight of a classroom! Still,
Liz Gentry, his son's teacher, was no battle-ax,
and soon Todd started planning some
extracurricular activities of his own....

September 1998
A CLASSIC ENCOUNTER
by Emilie Richards

Doctor Chris Matthews was intelligent, sexy
and *very* good with his hands—which made
him all the more dangerous to single mom
Lizette St. Hilaire. So how long could she
resist Chris's special brand of TLC?

Available at your favorite retail outlet!

MEN AT WORK™

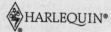 

Look us up on-line at: http://www.romance.net

PMAW2

SILHOUETTE® *Desire*

COMING NEXT MONTH